# Turnback Creek

# Turnback Creek

Lonnie Busch

Texas Review Press
Huntsville, Texas

Printed in the United States of America

FIRST EDITION, 2007

Requests for permission to reproduce material from this work should be sent to:

Permissions
Texas Review Press
English Department
Sam Houston State University
Huntsville, TX 77341-2146

**Turnback Creek is a work of fiction. Any similarity to actual persons, places, or events is purely coincidental and unintentional.**

**Library of Congress Cataloging-in-Publication Data**

Library of Congress Cataloging-in-Publication Data

Busch, Lonnie, 1952-
Turnback Creek / Lonnie Busch. -- 1st ed.
p. cm.
ISBN-13: 978-1-933896-07-6 (pbk. : alk. paper)
ISBN-10: 1-933896-07-8 (pbk. : alk. paper)
1. Brothers and sisters--Fiction. 2. Terminally ill--Fiction. 3. Terminal care--Fiction. 4. Bass fishing--Fiction. 5. Missouri--Fiction. I. Title.
PS3602.U837T87 2007
813'.6--dc22

2007018622

for my dad

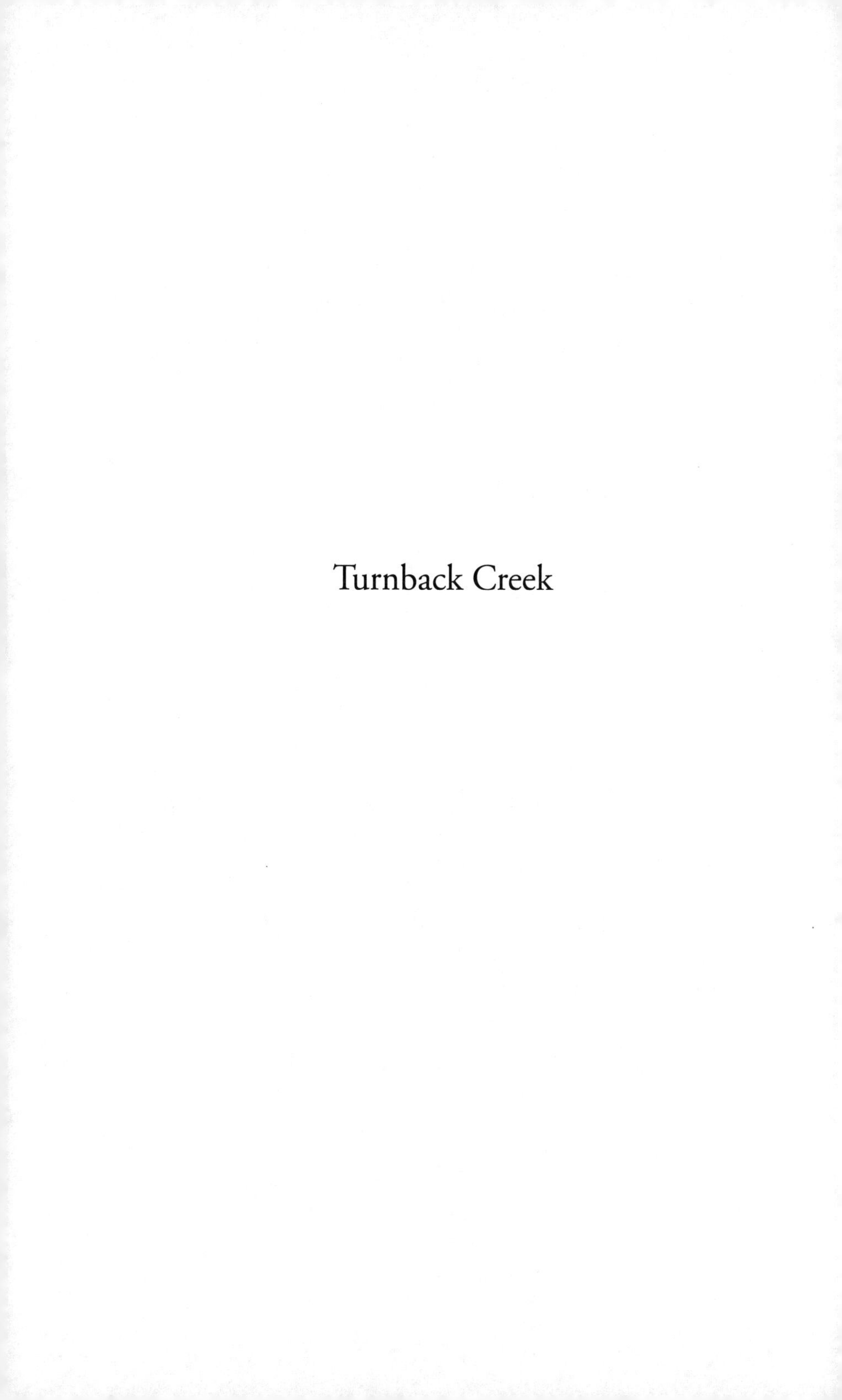

Turnback Creek

## *Chapter 1*

The reflection of the moon shattered when Cole's lure hit the water. He stared at the rings radiating out, at the moon slowly repairing itself on the black surface. Cole hated fishing on nights like this—when the bass weren't biting, the stillness so complete it seemed the world had stopped breathing—but night was the only time he had for himself.

Even the unexplainable breeze that always spread a faint ripple across the surface of Turnback Creek was oddly absent. Cole had just cocked his wrist to cast again when he heard a noise deep in the woods, a rumbling mechanical sound like a generator firing, a deep popping followed by a dull continuous thudding. He imagined one of those big Hollywood wind machines, the kind he'd seen on the MGM Studio tour out in California years ago, except that those fans weren't nearly as noisy as this contraption. This sound brought to mind a bulldozer, but he quickly ruled that out—no one would be crazy enough to drive a bulldozer in the dead of night. Not in the woods.

Using his trolling motor, Cole pointed his bass boat toward the commotion. Halfway across the cove, the noise stopped. Instinctively, he drew his foot from the pedal, as if to match the sudden silence, the boat drifting soundlessly through the darkness. He swept his gaze across the woods along the bank, the trees and foliage forming a black jagged wall. His eyes burned from lack of sleep and his back was sore from lifting Elsie. When the rumbling sprang to life again, he laid his fishing rod down and turned the boat toward the bank.

Tying off on a stump, he switched on his flashlight and headed up the rocky slope, his knees suddenly achy and stiff as he started the climb. Nearing the top, he stopped to catch his breath, then checked his watch. Almost two. He preferred to be off the lake by four, catch a few hours' sleep before Elsie woke. If he turned back now, he'd probably tally six hours. But the sound was too curious to ignore, even though it was foolhardy exploring the woods at night armed with only a flashlight.

The underbrush grew thicker as he picked his way up the steep bank, the mechanical thrumming louder, closer. It was definitely some kind of earthmoving equipment, he was sure of that now. He could hear the diesel engine grinding, and detected the faint smell of oil-fouled smoke. He knew that odor, had been around it all his life. He'd operated heavy equipment for over sixty years, driving a tractor as a young boy in Texas, then spending the rest of his adult life following government work to Louisiana, Kansas, Oklahoma, Nebraska, California, scraping out valleys to build dams, stripping trees from hillsides, gouging out highways and tunnels, pulling down white-collar money from the seat of a bulldozer, the sun turning his neck to jerky. There was no doubt the noise was some kind of earthmover.

When he reached the crest of the hill, he noticed a clearing through the cedars, moonlight coloring the open field a dusky blue. He switched off the flashlight and saw a backhoe loader trundling across ruts and bumps, bouncing stiffly on its hard suspension. Why would someone drive a piece of equipment like that, especially at night? Backhoe loaders were for digging, not joy riding. He recalled his dream of submerged bulldozers. In 1966 he helped move the Noble Church Cemetery in Louisiana, driving a bulldozer on the Toledo Bend Dam Project. He'd unearthed caskets dating back to the late 1800s, according to the records. A few years later, when the lake project was nearing completion, heavy spring rains flooded Toledo Bend faster than the Sabine River System officials expected. A few bulldozers were lost and still sat rusting at the bottom of the lake. Cole saw them in his dreams, the machines rumbling and belching blue smoke in the murky depths, the buckets scooping out empty caskets, no one at the controls.

Unlike his dream, someone was at the controls of this machine. When the loader turned toward him, he took a step back, deeper into the shadows. He wanted no trouble. When the machine rattled within forty feet of his hiding place, he spotted the driver perched up on the seat, but had a hard time trusting his eyes. Behind the wheel sat a skinny girl no more than thirteen or fourteen, with short black hair, and naked as a field mouse.

His breath caught. He couldn't turn away, couldn't stop looking at the child. Within twenty yards of the trees, the girl made a hard left and nearly flipped the rig, laughing like a lunatic. Cole couldn't hear her over the growl of the diesel, just saw her teeth flash white in the moonlight, her breasts jouncing between her skinny outstretched arms.

Before long, she parked the loader near the house on the hill, then climbed down and crossed the yard, her skin glowing like a projected image on a movie screen. She stopped at a lawn chair piled with clothing and began to dress. When she finished, she lit a cigarette and sat down, folding her knees to her chest, staring in Cole's direction. It was disconcerting, yet he was certain it was impossible for her to see him in the thicket. Nevertheless, he eased back, placing his shoe down softly, careful not to snap a twig. He was just about to squat down when she stood and started walking toward him.

Elsie said she felt like having breakfast outside on the deck. Cole stood at the stove stirring her oatmeal, looking at Elsie through the kitchen window, thinking about the girl. What if he hadn't fled the thicket? What if the girl had caught him spying? Last night he was relieved to have escaped undetected, but this morning, he almost wished he'd stayed, wondering if he would ever see her again. She was beautiful.

Cole heard Elsie yawn. With her eyes closed, head back, the breeze swirling the thin hairs around her face, she looked content. And with sunlight breathing life into her sunken features, it seemed as though she'd beaten her tumor overnight. But that's how it had been over the past few months. Elsie had a few good moments. This was one of them.

At her worst, she was unable to feed herself, or make it to the bathroom, sometimes soiling her clothes, but she refused to wear a diaper. Most of the time she shuffled around the house like a mechanical toy winding down, her skin thin as tissue, her veins prominent as exposed electrical wiring. On days like this, though, she seemed healthy as a washwoman, conversing, caring for herself, enjoying the sun. Cole knew the good moments had become less frequent over the past several weeks, but Elsie and he never discussed her decline.

He hadn't expected to outlive his wife Corinne. Now it looked as though he'd outlive his younger sister as well. At sixty-seven, Elsie already looked as though she'd weathered a hundred hard winters. During the day he cooked her meals, and washed up after her when she couldn't keep them down. He washed her clothes and cleaned her sheets, napped when she napped, and sat with her while she cried. At night, while Elsie drifted under the temporary reprieve of Sombien, Cole fished. It helped him to face the next day.

Cole turned the flame down and covered the oatmeal. Three months earlier, when she'd been diagnosed with a brain tumor, he sold his trailer in Oklahoma and moved to her home on Hardman Lake in the foothills of Missouri. There was no doubt she needed to be in the hospital up in Springfield, but she wanted to die in her own home, in her own bed, like her Herbert had a few years earlier.

Cole scooped the oatmeal into a bowl and carried it outside on a tray, placing it on the glass table next to Elsie's chair.

"Oatmeal never smells good, not like fresh bacon or honey-baked ham," Elsie said. "I see you remembered the syrup today."

Cole had never forgotten to put syrup on her oatmeal—he knew that's how she liked it. His only crime had been stirring it in once, thinking she'd like it mixed. She had insisted he forgot to add it. From then on he made sure to drizzle it on top so she could see it.

"Why don't you sit?" Elsie said.

"I need to wash the pan before the oatmeal sets up. It's like concrete when it dries."

"Oh, you're so dramatic, Cole. All you have to do is soak the pan if that happens. You men. A woman would never worry about such a thing."

Cole knew that wasn't true—Corinne never let food sit in her pots and pans. He pulled out the chair and took his eyes to the lake. He was glad Elsie was able to feed herself today, but didn't really want to sit and chat. He had a thousand chores and wanted to get a nap so he'd be rested for the night.

"I want you to fix the spare bed for Lily and Thomas," Elsie said. "We'll put Lionel on the foldout couch."

Cole ignored her. She often imagined guests, or recalled past visits as future events. Then he remembered that his daughter was arriving tomorrow. That's why Elsie was doing so well today. He'd noticed that whenever company was scheduled, Elsie perked up, seemed less needy, less sick, as if the promise of visitors gave her a slight edge over death. He was relieved at first, knowing Lily would shoulder most of the burden of taking care of Elsie, keeping her company during the day. Lily loved Elsie and they always got along well. The discouraging part was knowing he'd be saddled with Thomas and Lionel. They'd want to go fishing and he'd have to entertain them. He didn't mind his grandson, but his son-in-law, Thomas, believed he knew everything about fishing, even though he'd only been a few times in his life. And after having them out all day on the lake, Cole would have little strength to go back out at night. He relied on his nightly excursions, especially now, and thought about the young girl. He wasn't sure if it was a sexual attraction or just a curiosity. After all, she hadn't looked much older than his grandson, Lionel. And it had been over ten years since he'd been with a woman—his wife, Corinne—and had all but forgotten about carnal desire, and more than that, hadn't really cared. The urgency had left. Until last night. Now he couldn't stop picturing the girl, her thin arms, her small breasts, her white skin. He wondered what color her eyes were. Her hair had looked black in the moonlight, but it could have been any dark shade, could even have been the color of turmeric, the color of Corinne's hair.

"I'm speaking to you, Cole. You look like you need a nap. Where are you?"

"Thinking about everything I got to do today, Elsie."

"You'll have plenty of time to get everything done. They won't get here until late tomorrow afternoon. You know how Thomas is, stopping at every roadside attraction along the way. I'll never forget the trip I took with them to Arizona after my Herbert died. It was just horrible. I thought it was going to take us six months to get from Kansas City to Phoenix."

"You want coffee, Elsie?" Cole asked, getting up from the table.

"No. I don't think I can eat any more oatmeal, either. Would you take this tray inside so it doesn't draw flies? Oh, and I need you to pick up my prescription."

Cole took the tray inside and washed the dishes. He put everything away, then straightened up the living room and folded the newspapers Elsie thumbed through but never really read. Elsie yelled something from the deck.

"What say, Elsie?" Cole asked, walking to the door and speaking through the screen.

"Did you catch any fish last night?"

"No, it was real slow." He wasn't really lying. Fishing had been slow up until he'd hiked up the bank and spotted the girl.

"Well, next time you catch some, bring them in so we can cook them. Herbert always brought in his fish. We ate fresh fish all the time. I thought you liked fish."

"Do you get scared, Elsie? At night, when I go out fishing?"

Elsie smiled, shook her head. "That's the only time I'm not scared, Cole. My sleep medicine makes me like anyone else. In my dreams I'm never sick."

Cole had asked her before, feeling guilty about his nightly outings, and she always told him he needed them, that he couldn't stay penned up with her twenty-four hours a day.

"I'm going to town. Need anything else?" Cole asked.

"Maybe some cookies, Fig Newtons or something. And a sack of those miniature Milky Ways Lionel likes so much. That one Halloween he sat and ate a whole bowl of them by himself. I thought Lily was going to kill him." Elsie laughed, then started coughing. "Bring me a blanket, will you, Cole?"

Cole thought about driving to Mountain View to see if he could find where the girl lived. How many houses could there be with a backhoe loader in the yard? He even thought he might recognize the house by its shutters. She had to live in Mountain View. It was the closest town to Turnback Creek, but he had no idea how far off Route MM the house might be. Homes around there were miles off the main roads.

He made a left onto 74 and crossed the bridge. He could see the mouth of Turnback Creek, a pontoon boat motoring past the point, smoke pouring from the barbecue grill on the front deck. Off the opposite point sat a bass boat, two fishermen standing, casting toward the bank. A pleasure boat with two couples in bathing suits sped beneath the bridge, then popped out on the other side. By day, Turnback was no different than any other arm of the lake—sparkling water and pea-gravel banks—but at night it was a queer and puzzling place with the faint steady breeze issuing from its headwaters, rippling the surface even when the rest of the lake was flat as plate glass. And no sounds. Not a peeper, cricket, nightjar, or owl. But the fishing was usually too good in Turnback for him to be discouraged by ghosts. That's what he imagined when he felt the cool breeze at night—ghosts.

Modern folks might have thought the fear irrational, but not Cole. Hardman Reservoir was an impoundment like any other impoundment, created by flooding thousands of acres of house foundations, roads, and farms, and at least a few cemeteries. Even though the Corps of Engineers made every effort to move the graves, Cole wondered about the spiritual impact of such an undertaking. He wondered if the Turnback Creek arm of Hardman might have had a plot or two that had gone forgotten or just plain overlooked.

Cole made a left on Highway 89 toward Pilot Gap. Most of the towns around Hardman Reservoir had grown a great deal in the fifteen years since Elsie and Herbert had bought the lake house. Pilot Gap was now home to three new video stores, a Pizza Hut, the Second Time thrift shop, a DB gas station, Vivian's Beauty Salon, at least three new churches, and a recycling center. There was talk of a Wal-Mart to be built a few miles outside the city limits on 89.

Cole parked in front of the Pilot Pharmacy. After getting Elsie's prescription, he walked to Kearnes Market and bought Fig Newtons and candy bars. He couldn't remember if he was supposed to buy Milky Ways or Milk Duds, so he bought a bag of each. He carried the sacks to his truck, then stopped at the Pilot Diner.

Margie brought him a cup of coffee. "How's Elsie?" she asked, leaning over, elbows on the counter.

"Perked up a little," he said, remembering the seventeen different prescriptions he'd counted on Elsie's nightstand. He was convinced her worsening condition stemmed more from the combination of drugs than the tumor, keeping her sick all the time. He'd insisted she call the doctor about all the medication, but she'd refused flatly, telling him the doctor knew a lot more than he did.

"That's good," Margie said.

"Lily's coming tomorrow," Cole told her, unsure why he mentioned it, his mind on the girl.

Margie patted Cole's hand. "That'll give you a little break. You look like you need it. Can I get you some eggs and bacon?"

Cole shook his head and said he wasn't hungry. When she started to walk away, he said, "You used to live over in Mountain View, didn't you?"

She nodded, pulling a piece of pie from the circular glass case for another customer. "Why?"

"You know much about Turnback Creek?"

"I fished it with Ben a few times. But, hell, you know this lake better than Ben. He doesn't know dick about fishing."

"I was wondering who owns that land up there in Turnback, you know, where that old rusted thresher sits on the bank?"

"I don't know anything about any thresher, but I can tell you if it's land you're interested in up in Turnback, Hannah Pelton's who you need to talk with. She owns all the acreage around there."

"What's the address?"

Margie's expression went dry, her eyes fixed on his. He wished he'd eased the question into the conversation with more tact, hadn't dropped it like a copperhead. He thought it might be easy to get information, but this was far more complicated than he wanted. "Doesn't matter." Cole picked up his coffee and sipped it, hoping she would deliver the pie she was still holding.

"I don't know, Cole. You interested in buying land down here? I thought you'd just live at Elsie's if you decided to stay."

"I was thinking about an investment, that's all."

"I'm sure she's not selling," Margie said. "I heard she was building a new home next to her old one. I don't think she'd ever sell any part of her land, likes her privacy too much. Lives alone. Keeps to herself. Doesn't even go into town anymore. Has all her groceries delivered, the way I heard it."

"She have children?" he said. Margie's eyebrows shot up. Cole felt a tinge of guilt, as if he'd gone too far—Hannah Pelton having children had nothing to do with his supposed interest in her land. After a moment her features relaxed. She twisted her mouth to one side. "Has a son, I think. Doesn't come around anymore, though. Went in the Army years ago and never came back."

Cole wondered if the son was dead. Margie seemed to read his expression.

"He didn't get killed or nothing like that," she said. "Just didn't come around anymore. Least that's what folks say."

"How about a daughter, or granddaughter?"

"Don't believe so. Just Hannah. But I ain't lived over there for a long time. I have a friend knows everything about everyone in Mountain View. She's the one to talk to. Let me deliver this pie and I'll call her up, put you in touch—then you can tell me what this is really about."

"No," Cole said, putting a dollar and some quarters on the counter. "Won't be necessary. I've got to get back. Elsie'll be worried."

Margie was setting down the pie when Cole shot out the door and hurried to his truck. He spun his tires a little as he pulled from the parking spot and felt like he was doing something illegal. If not illegal, certainly underhanded, wrong. "How stupid can you be, Cole Emerson?" He slapped his palms on the steering wheel, his eyes wired to the yellow line running down the center of the road.

## *Chapter 2*

Lily had called while he was in town and said they would be arriving early, sometime tonight, but not to wait up because it would be after one in the morning. Cole listened as Elsie told him the news, his chest tightening, his mind plotting a plan to get up to Turnback Creek. He could go after Elsie went to bed and come in at midnight. That would give him at least two hours.

"Evidently Lily did all the driving and Thomas slept most of the trip, so they only stopped for gas and food. I could never live with that man. When he sleeps he snores. When he's awake, he never stops talking. Are you going to run the sweeper?"

Cole nodded, the conversation at the diner coming back like the drip of a slow faucet. Hannah lived alone. Hannah was most likely old, but Cole couldn't figure out why he knew that. Maybe she wasn't old, but that certainly wasn't Hannah driving the backhoe loader. Maybe that girl didn't even belong to Hannah. Maybe she didn't belong anywhere, some kind of vagrant, maybe, or one of those backpackers he'd pass from time to time on the highway headed for Springfield.

"Are you going to sweep now, Cole? I need to lie down. You know how the sweeper keeps me awake."

"I'll do it right now. Go on in and lay down. Your color looks better today, Elsie."

"I feel better, although my tummy's a little upset. Probably just tired. Could you make tea? That always seems to settle my stomach. Don't forget the milk and honey." Elsie leaned over and kissed him on the cheek. "I always forget to thank you for everything you do for me, Cole. You won't have to do it much longer. I can feel it."

"Now don't talk like that, Elsie. I'll bring your tea." He turned on the television and closed the door so she wouldn't hear the sweeper.

Elsie was already asleep when Cole came back with the tea. He set it on her nightstand, more as proof that he'd brought it than anything else—he knew she'd never drink it cold. He ran the sweeper and thought about the girl. Would he sneak up through the woods again, watch her ride naked through the field? Did he plan to talk to her, or just spy on her? It sounded horrible in his head. Last night was innocent—he'd just followed the sound. Tonight was planned, unforgivable.

As he stretched new sheets on the bed in the spare room, he realized that all his thoughts were about the girl, that she was the force propelling him through his chores, that if he didn't get back to Turnback Creek, he'd be disappointed. He couldn't recall the last time he'd felt disappointment over anything. There hadn't been anything to be let down about in a long time. Even so, he knew if he went, he'd feel ashamed. He'd never thought of himself as someone capable of such a deplorable act, and would have condemned any man considering such a thing. That always seemed the way, he thought—judging other folks' demons only served to bring out your own.

He pushed the pillows into the pillowcases, making sure they were on straight, then arranged them at the head of the bed. He tightened the spread at the corners, working out the wrinkles on top of the pillows, a nice crease beneath. He straightened the rug under the rocker.

When he finished cleaning the spare bathroom, he placed an extra roll of paper on the tank of the toilet. In some untilled region of his mind, he figured that all his caregiving and do-gooding might earn him some shrift if his family found out what he was up to, make them think he was a fine man in spite of his unspeakable actions. In the part of his brain that served him on a daily basis, he knew his virtuous deeds wouldn't matter beans if Lily or Elsie found out what he was up to. They'd find it unpardonable. And Corinne, if she were alive, would suffer ruinous humiliation.

Cole went to the kitchen and put a pot of bean soup on, then turned the flame to low. He started a load of laundry and tossed Elsie's nightgown and underwear in with the sheets, even though she'd instructed him to wash them separately, and wash her panties by hand. It was enough that he hand-washed her bras in the kitchen sink—and felt stupid doing it. He wasn't about to clean her underwear the same way. Nothing he owned needed to be washed by hand, he thought, except his dang hands and pecker. He felt himself growing angry. He went to the fridge, took out a beer, and sat at the kitchen table. He tilted the can back, the beer burning his throat. He screwed his knuckles into his eye sockets, trying to rub away the stinging. When he opened them, he peered across the lake. Two crappie fishermen were working the vertical rock face along the far bluff. Cole stared at them, the men looking as tiny and useless as a picture in a magazine ad.

Elsie was having a bad evening. Cole helped her from the bath and was starting to towel off her back when she spun away and dropped at the toilet. Cole tried to get a rug between her bare knees and the hard tile floor so she wouldn't be so uncomfortable, but the spell hit her too quickly. She heaved and gagged and cried and Cole felt helpless, something hard squeezing inside him. He placed a cold washcloth on the back of her neck and covered her naked shoulders with a dry towel. He combed his fingers through her thinning hair, gently caressing her scalp. She knelt a long time, praying out loud for God to take her, forgive her, crying, pleading, and Cole found himself praying along with her, silently.

Her skin had stopped looking like flesh and Cole couldn't even describe it in his own mind. He half expected the inside of her mouth to be black, like that salmon he'd seen in the Kalamazoo River laboriously finning along the surface, dying after the spawn, devoured from the inside out by its own stomach acid. That's what he imagined happening to Elsie, being eaten up from the inside out till there would be nothing left of her but a shell. He wondered if he should stay in, if this was the night she'd die. But there had been many nights much worse than this. She turned to face him, her eyes dark and puffy, her hair sweat-soaked and plastered to her forehead.

"Help me to bed, Cole."

Her body wobbled as he pulled her up by her armpits. He was surprised at how heavy she was without the help of her legs, even though she weighed less than a hundred pounds now. He got her into bed, brought her a glass of water for her medicine. While she swallowed her pills, he rummaged her dresser for a nightgown. She sat on the edge of the bed as he slipped it over her head and gently guided her arms into the sleeves. Bird bones, he thought, fearing he might snap her wrists if he gripped them too tightly.

"Lay down and I'll slip these on," Cole said, pulling a pair of underpants from the dresser.

"I don't need those tonight. Switch the television on, will you, Cole?"

Cole thumbed the remote, then placed it on the nightstand by her glass of water. She was lying on her back staring at the ceiling, through it, it seemed to Cole. Her lips were moving, as if she were mouthing words, tears filling her eyes.

"What's wrong, Elsie?"

She never looked over, never looked anywhere but at the ceiling. "God will never forgive me. Can't you see that, Cole? God won't let me die—and won't let me heal." She started shaking, first her head, then her entire body. He grabbed the comforter and pulled it up over her chest, thinking she was cold. She moaned and shook her head, spit foaming between her lips.

"Elsie. You got to relax." He sat on the bed next to her, resting his hand on her shoulder. After a moment, the harsh shadows on her face softened, her closed eyelids turning smooth as waxed paper. The drugs had finally taken hold. He got up slowly, then went in and flushed the toilet again. He scrubbed the bathroom, listening to see if she'd start coughing. After twenty minutes or so, he knew she was asleep. He put a pot of coffee on, checked on her once more before filling his thermos, then crept out the front door.

The sky was bruised and dark, smelling of rain. He fired the outboard, switched on the running lights, and idled out past the end of the dock, pushing the throttle forward when he hit open water. The fiberglass hull of his Ranger lifted from the water smooth as a jet. In seconds, Cole was cruising across the black polished surface of Hardman Lake, the warm breeze rushing across his face, sweeping away all the sounds and odors of disease.

In less than fifteen minutes Cole was guiding his bass boat under the Highway 74 Bridge, veering toward the mouth of Turnback Creek. The hum of the outboard was comforting, flushing the past two hours from his head. In minutes he was in sight of the rusted thresher. He backed off the throttle till the hull settled into the water with the grace of a landing mallard, then crawled the boat to within fifty feet of shore.

Turnback Creek was different in the deep black of a moonless night. He switched his running lights off to allow his eyes to adjust to the dark. Sixty yards ahead on the right sat the thresher. Even that looked different, farther up the bank, as if it had been moved. When Cole shut off the engine, the heavy silence of the creek sat like dew on everything. The previous evening suddenly seemed like it hadn't happened, or was off in the future, as if he'd imagined tying his boat to a stump, hiking up the hill. Standing, he surveyed the area, then walked to the front deck of his boat and gently lifted the trolling motor by the cord and slid it into the water. Even though Cole felt no breeze, the water rippled and lapped gently against the fiberglass hull. Using the motor, he guided the boat toward the thresher on the bank and thought maybe this would be a better night for fishing than spying.

When he coasted within four feet of the stump, he eased the trolling motor out of the water and into its cradle, then knelt on the deck and placed his palm against the stump so the bow wouldn't crash into the bank. He tied off and headed up the slope.

Shining the flashlight on the ground, he picked his way through brambles and chokeberry bushes, limbs scratching across his cheeks and ears. He tried to protect his eyes with his forearm, each clumsy footfall sounding like a gunshot in the solid silence. He tried to step more deftly, but there seemed no quiet route for size twelve boots.

From the edge of the thicket he could see the house and the backhoe loader. He switched his flashlight off and slid it into his pocket. The backhoe loader sat motionless as a praying mantis. Now what? he thought. Just stand there till something happens? In that moment, he wasn't sure what he'd been hoping for. Certainly he wanted to see the girl again, but why? What had he planned to do? He hadn't thought it out that far and felt foolish. He was just about to pull his flashlight out and start back down the hill when someone blinded him with a light.

"I don't know what you're up to, mister, but you better freeze where you stand."

Cole hesitated, raising his left forearm to shield his eyes from the glare. He recalled Margie saying that Hannah Pelton kept to herself, that she had a son, and that her land wasn't for sale. This voice was definitely a woman's.

"Who are you?" she asked.

Cole heard the unmistakable click of a hammer being drawn back. The woman eased her arm out, the barrel pointed at him, glistening in the beam from her flashlight.

"I meant no harm. I was just . . . ," Cole said, his mind reeling with ridiculous lies, none of which reached his lips. The bones in his legs felt weak and he thought he might collapse. It had been a long time since his courage had been tested. Not since the barroom brawls in Louisiana, since the drunken fistfights after driving a bulldozer all day under a scorching Texas sun. Somewhere along the way it had wilted. Yet in all that time no one had ever stuck a gun in his face, at least not anyone with enough cause and right to shoot him.

"You come up here to take a crap on my land?" the woman said, her voice sounding more youthful.

Cole was thankful for the excuse, but hesitated to take advantage of it. How would she feel about him defecating on her property? Violated? Disgusted? Would that anger her enough to shoot him? Maybe she was crazy. "No, ma'am. I . . . ." The sentence died. He couldn't think of one good reason to be up in those woods, at least one that wouldn't get him shot. "Must have had a weak spot in my line," he finally said toward the bright light. "My crank bait snapped right off on the cast. Landed somewhere up here." Although he had no idea where the lie came from, it sounded credible, at least to his ears. That very thing had happened on several occasions. He pointed toward the weeds, as if that's where his lure might have landed. She swung her flashlight at the weeds, then back in his eyes before he could get a look at her.

"You weren't even fishing," she said. "From where I sat, you just pulled right up and tied off, like you had a purpose."

If she shot him, how would he explain it to the doctors? Or Elsie? Or Lily? And that's if he lived. What if she kept shooting him? He'd never been shot before, not even in the Korean War.

"Ms. Pelton?" he said. "Hannah Pelton?"

The words hung in the silence between him and the bright light.

"How do you know my name?" the woman asked.

"A feller told me you had some land for sale, said you owned a few hundred acres up and down Turnback Creek."

"Folks say all kinds of crap that ain't true. Just like you're doing now."

"Look, ma'am, I'm very sorry. I'll just be on my way. I'll never bother you again."

He turned and started walking down the hill toward his boat, trying to hold his calm, stepping lightly so as not to upset the rocks or dirt, as if any disturbance could set her off, cause her to start shooting.

Thirty feet from his boat, a sharp, loud clap to the back of his head sent him to his knees. Colors thundered through his skull, red, then black, then white, small explosions. At first he thought he'd been shot, except he hadn't heard the pop of a round. The pain focused tightly, racing deep inside his head, spreading across his scalp, down his arms. He dug his fingers into his hair and brought them out bloodied. He spun around on the ground, trying to get his bearings, bracing himself for another blow. The woman shined the light on the rocks in front of him, on the drops of blood.

"You okay, mister?"

There was no compassion in her voice. Cole nodded, pushing to his feet, trembling. He wiped his bloody fingers on his jeans. The pain thumped at his head with the cadence of a heartbeat.

"I meant to catch you in the back of your jacket with that rock, mister. Didn't mean to draw blood."

He was angry now, and frightened, the gun barrel dazzling in her flashlight beam.

"I figured out what you were doing up here," she said. "You wanted to get another look at me naked. Ain't that right?"

It was the girl. Cole wasn't sure if the truth would get him out of this, but lying hadn't worked. He explained how he'd been fishing the previous night when he'd heard a sound coming from the woods, that he'd gone up to explore, see if someone needed help. He told her it was too dark to really see anything except the backhoe loader bouncing across the field. Too far to see who was driving.

"You and the truth seem to be strangers to each other," she said. "You saw me naked, at least my chest." She swept the light back and forth across his face as if she were trying to erase his features with the beam of light. "It's only fair I see you."

Cole took a step back. He wasn't about to take his clothes off. She could just shoot him, or hit him with rocks till he was dead.

"Not your pants, mister. Just your shirt. Lord knows I don't care nothing about what you got in your jeans."

He spun away from her, loping down the hill toward his boat, stopping when he heard the crack of her gun. It sounded as if the night sky had blown apart, the bullet ripping into the ground two feet to his right. Looking where the round had buried in the earth, he wondered whether she was a good shot or a bad one. He heard her walk up behind him, a small avalanche of dirt and stones marking her approach.

"Take it off."

Cole unbuttoned his shirt, then slid it off and held it at his side.

"Now the undershirt."

He removed his undershirt and stood with his back to her. What would Corinne think? Never had he felt so humiliated.

"Turn around."

He eased around slowly, facing her, then the light.

"All your chest hairs are white. Like little duck feathers."

Cole was embarrassed, not so much by his nakedness, but by the youth and exuberance in her voice, as if growing old had been some kind of failure on his part.

The girl stepped closer. "Can I touch it?"

## *Chapter 3*

Lily's Land Rover sat in the driveway behind his truck, hemming it in. The house was dark. Cole touched the light function on his watch. Three twenty-five. He hoped no one was awake.

The kitchen floor squeaked and groaned as he padded toward the hallway. He'd decided to enter from the back deck, use the slider, make less noise. Halfway across the living room he heard Lionel stir on the sleeper-sofa.

"Catch any fish, Grandpa?"

Cole looked over. Lionel sat up, his fists in his eyes, trying to rub them open. "Go back to sleep, Lionel." Cole walked over and kissed the boy on the forehead, remembering how the girl's small hand had caressed his chest, her fingers combing through the fine white hairs. Lionel was only a couple years younger than she was, but so different. Cole couldn't figure out what the dissimilarity was, other than the obvious: Hannah was a girl. Lionel fell back into the blankets and rolled on his side. Cole touched the boy's head, then stole back to his own bedroom and closed the door.

He needed a shave but was too weary to stand at the mirror and face himself. He undressed and rolled in between the sheets, thinking about Hannah, her sapling-thin arms, her reed-slim wrists. She was probably the same size Elsie was now, though Elsie had been a robust woman before she'd gotten ill. But Hannah wasn't fragile like Elsie, her bones in danger of crumbling from the mere act of standing, as if the weight of her skull had grown too heavy for her skeleton. Cole always worried that Elsie would collapse in a pile of bone dust. It was a horrible image.

Cole turned on his side to look out the window, thinking about Hannah's hand on his chest, her saying how the hairs tickled her palm when she touched them lightly. She had smirked—not at him, but maybe at the novelty of time, how it turned things white and dry and useless.

She'd walked past him down the bank while he'd pulled his shirt on. She had climbed into his boat, lifted compartment lids, thrown herself into the driver's seat.

"I've never been in a boat before," she said.

They sat in his boat a long time, mostly her talking, him wondering what he was doing there. She told him how she'd been living in Anchorage with her father, who was in the military, that her parents were separated, that she'd come to stay with her grandmother until her father came to get her. She was going to start school in Mountain View in the fall. "Can't be much worse than the one I went to in Anchorage."

"My daddy used to run off all the time, leave us alone," Cole said, hoping to find common ground with the girl. "He'd be gone a few weeks, sometimes a month. When he came home, he'd always bring Elsie and me something from the city, some kind of special candy we'd never had before. One day he ran off and never came back."

"That's an interesting story, mister," Hannah had said a bit sharply, "but my daddy didn't run off. He's coming back for me as soon as he gets leave. He's a military man. Maybe if your daddy had been a military man he'd have had more courage to do what he was supposed to do."

Cole thought maybe she was right. He'd never wasted much energy thinking about his father, just assumed the old man had grease on his soles and couldn't stay put in one place very long.

Cole had watched ripples purl across the water past the hull, then looked over at the girl. She had her jeans rolled up to her knees, her shoes and socks sitting on the floor. Her legs were white as almonds and just as smooth.

"Take me for a ride, Cole."

Hannah had wanted to ride on the front deck.

Cole told her it wasn't safe, but she insisted. He drove out Turnback Creek and headed up the lake. The water was polished ebony. Without warning, Hannah spun around and yelled. He jerked back on the throttle under the 74 bridge and came to a stop. "Turn off the motor," Hannah said, pointing toward the cars going over the bridge above them. He twisted the key. "Listen how they echo," she said. "I love that sound. Like a huge spaceship or something." The kid part of her surprised him, jolted him back to the truth of the situation, that she was a child. She could have been Lionel talking about one of his computer games. Yet Cole couldn't help but see her as a young woman—nineteen, twenty-one—but maybe that was for the sake of his conscience, or his devil, he wasn't sure which. Hannah stretched out on the front deck of his boat, listening to cars headed home after the taverns closed.

"Doesn't your grandmother worry about you?" Cole asked.

"She has pills that keep her from worry."

Cole turned away from the window and faced the wall of his bedroom, picturing Hannah sprawled across the front of his boat, her arms outstretched, pretending to grab the cars as they went by. He was tired, tired of thinking about the girl, tired of taking care of Elsie, tired of being old. When he finally fell asleep, he slept hard, trapped in dreams. Bulldozers rumbled past him, digging up graves in the barn where he and Elsie had stacked hay bales as kids and fed their horses, Duke and Candy Bar. One bulldozer unearthed a coffin and carried it out the barn doors just as another came in the opposite entrance carrying a coffin, dumping it in the freshly dug hole. The barn started filling with water, the dirt floor turning to mud. A mat of straw floated above his head as the water rose. The bulldozers continued all night long, taking out coffins, bringing in new ones, no one at the controls. In the dream he could breathe under water, but couldn't get out of the barn, or stop the bulldozers.

The next morning he woke more exhausted than if

he'd not slept at all. And by the ache in his jaw he knew he'd been grinding his teeth.

It was near noon according to the clock on his dresser. He couldn't remember a time in his life he'd slept so late and so poorly. He dressed and checked on Elsie. She was still asleep. That seemed odd. The house was quiet and stuffy. He fully expected to see Lionel sitting on the family room floor watching television, and Thomas to be out on the deck reading a financial magazine.

Lily came out of the bathroom wrapped in her robe, her hair wet and stringy. She was wearing it short now and it shot up off her scalp like a brush fire.

"Did you have a good drive, Lily?"

"Yeah, Daddy. Real good."

She rushed past him as if he were a ghost. He knew she was upset, not so much by her brusque manner as by the way her green eyes darkened to the point where they were almost without color.

"How could you, Daddy?" she said, spinning toward him. "How could you leave Aunt Elsie alone last night? When we came in, she was sitting up in bed sobbing, crying out gibberish. What the hell is going on?"

"Was she awake?"

Lily turned toward the kitchen, scrubbing the towel into her hair again. "I don't think so."

"That's how it's been, Lily." He followed her through the house, tucking his shirt in. "If you leave her alone, she goes back to sleep."

"I made coffee. Do you want a cup?"

Cole nodded and sat at the kitchen table, looking out at the lake. Elsie's home sat on a bluff overlooking the King's River arm of Hardman Reservoir. Miles of lake spread out north and south like a vast shiny blue ribbon. Lily set the coffee down in front of him and went back to the stove.

"Where's Thomas and Lionel?" he asked.

"Fishing off the dock."

Lily sat down and crossed her legs, sipping her coffee. "Last night, when I was trying to help Aunt Elsie get back to sleep, she kept repeating something over and over, Daddy."

"What?"

"She said, 'Push me, Cole. Come on, push me!'"

Cole agreed to take Thomas and Lionel to Pilot Gap for lunch, give Lily some time alone with Elsie. Thomas, his arm around Lionel in the front seat of Cole's pickup, started talking about a new theory on structure fishing, obviously something he'd recently read in a fishing magazine. "If we could find some old flooded mills on the map . . . " Thomas was saying, but Cole couldn't concentrate, figuring a way back to Turnback Creek at night without Thomas and Lionel, and without upsetting Lily. He had promised Hannah he'd be there. "Don't let me down, Cole Emerson," she'd told him. He could still see her climbing the hill, disappearing into the woods, the pistol dangling from her skinny arm like a Christmas ornament that was too big for its branch.

Cole stopped at the tackle store so Thomas and Lionel could buy fishing licenses. Maybe he could tell Thomas he knew of an old mill, take them up to some spot in the King's River arm. Thomas wouldn't know the difference. He would believe whatever Cole told him. The main thing was to keep them out all afternoon in the sun, wear them down so they wouldn't want to night fish.

Thomas grinned as he stepped from the tackle store, his hand on Lionel's back, a paper sack clutched to his chest. The new bounce in Thomas's step made Cole uneasy. It wasn't that Thomas was usually grim or anything, but he possessed a cool restraint that stood out amongst rural folks, an urban superiority that Cole had learned to tolerate over the years.

"Forget flooded mills, Dad!" Thomas said, scooting across the front seat after Lionel got in. "I've got something better."

Cole didn't like when Thomas called him "Dad." And he especially didn't like the "something better," whatever it was. Thomas became a tenacious bloodhound when he wanted the current fishing report, accosting anyone who wore a fishing cap or towed a boat. "What lure you catching them on? Where? How deep? How many? How big?" He'd turn on the false-friendly that made him so successful at his brokerage firm, treating the lake area as his own backwoods amusement park, the inhabitants as his personal attendants. It was embarrassing and Cole hated to be around him when he wheedled information.

Driving to the diner, Cole tried to listen as Thomas explained what the tackle store owner had told him. Supposedly, a couple fishermen from Mountain View caught over twenty bass up to five pounds in one night. "All on these black spinner baits. Show Grandpa, Lionel." The bag crinkled as Lionel pulled one of the plastic-wrapped packages from the bag.

"See, Grandpa."

Cole glanced from the road, fixing the image of the new lure in his mind, but mostly regarding Lionel's thin wrist, his even, slender fingers, youthful and smooth as bone, like Hannah's.

They sat at the counter and ordered. While they waited for their lunch, Thomas detailed the technique the fishermen had used. "They threw their spinner baits right up on the bank and dragged them back into the water," Thomas told Cole, describing how the store owner had said the fish were in less than two feet of water. Thomas told Lionel they would need to take a nap when they got back to the house so they'd be ready to fish all night, asked him if he brought warm clothes, said that it could get cold when the dew settled. Something inside Cole flagged at the thought of not seeing Hannah—he needed to see her. *Needed*? Cole wasn't sure when that had happened, when seeing Hannah had become so crucial, had become requisite.

Just as Cole was about to explain to Thomas that the fishing hadn't been so good the last few nights, that conditions changed quickly in late spring and the fishing report was probably no longer accurate, he noticed a couple in the booth by the window. The man, who was slumped forward in his seat, had his back to Cole, but the woman looked familiar. When he studied her further, he could see she wasn't a woman at all, just a girl. Hannah. Cole was almost certain of it, even though he'd never seen her in the light. But he recognized her by something other than her features, something in the way she held her head, or the way she moved her arms, or let her back sag slightly, the way one would recognize someone across a street or in a crowded auditorium.

He caught himself staring, wondering if she'd seen him, if she'd recognized him. She was more beautiful than he'd remembered, her features round and soft, her hair the color of strong coffee. Using her fork, she sawed off a corner of her waffle, swirled it in syrup and brought it to her lips. She never looked up and only occasionally glanced over at the man opposite her. His hair was cut short on the sides, longer on top, a small bald spot shining through his thinning hair like a white stone in a creek bed. He was motionless, bent forward, as if he'd fallen asleep sitting up. Maybe it was her father come to take her back to Anchorage. But he wasn't supposed to come for a couple of weeks. From the back, Cole thought the man looked military.

The girl cut another section of waffle and was raising it to her lips when she glanced over at Cole. Cole held her eyes for a moment, but detected no flicker of recognition in them. She turned away just as smoothly, bringing the bite to her mouth, her eyes fixed on something outside.

Margie set plates down in front of Cole, Lionel and Thomas. When Lionel got up to use the bathroom, Thomas turned toward Cole and started talking about places to night fish, explaining that the tackle shop owner had told him pea gravel banks were the best. Cole bit into his turkey sandwich, nodding at Thomas, thinking about the girl, suddenly anxious over the fact that she might recognize him, might walk up to the counter and say, "Hi, Cole." How would he explain the familiarity to Thomas? What if she mentioned their boat ride? Or his promise to return?

He pulled his cap down and swiveled a quarter-turn away from her booth, raising his elbows to the counter, letting his head sink down into his shoulders. An unbearable guilt rose inside him, the hiding making him feel like a slug. He was too old for this. But when would it have been acceptable? He tried to convince himself he did nothing wrong, just gave a girl a ride in his boat. That was it. But that was a lie too. Plenty had happened inside him. A long-dormant yearning had been resuscitated. And it was consuming him.

"So this is your grandson?"

Cole looked up from his green beans to see Stu Rainy, the owner of the diner, hovering behind the counter. Stu's apron was grease splattered and burnished gray where he constantly wiped his hands across his round belly. Stu dragged his palms across the same spot before placing them on the counter. "Fine looking boy, Cole. You must be proud. And this must be his father."

Thomas shook Stu's hand and told him Lionel was in the seventh grade. Thomas was saying something to Stu, but Cole couldn't follow the conversation, bothered over his name being spoken out loud. If the girl in the booth were Hannah, she surely would have heard Stu call him "Cole," removing all doubt. He hoped Stu would let it drop, shuffle back to the grill to burn more ground beef, but he stood there, towering over them, and Cole knew what was coming next.

"So, Cole, you been catching 'em at night?"

"Kind of slow lately," Cole said in a low voice, but the diner seemed unusually quiet, the slick blue walls amplifying small sounds, and Cole could hear a fork tinkling against a plate in the booth behind him, could almost feel Hannah's breath on his neck.

"Boys been coming in here saying they're really getting 'em after dark, Cole. Can't imagine you not having any luck, good a fisherman as you are."

"It's just been a little off." At this, Cole heard something crash to the floor behind him. Everyone spun toward the commotion. The man in the booth had knocked his coffee cup to the floor.

"Don't you folks move now! Let me get that glass up," Stu said, rushing around the counter with a broom and dustpan. Thomas wiped his hand across his pants where coffee had splashed up on him. When the man tried to stand, he became wobbly, falling against the table and back into the seat, as if he had bounced there. Cole could tell he was drunk. The dishes rattled and clinked when the man tried to stand again, using the table to push himself up. The way the table leaned, Cole expected the rest of the dishes to end up on the floor.

Stu swept the glass into the dustpan, telling the man to stay put. The man grumbled something while the girl sat still, staring at Cole. Cole tried to read her eyes, and thought he saw a glimmer of recognition, or disdain, but she looked away, standing when Stu finished with the mess. She took some bills out of the pocket of her jeans and dropped them on the table, then took the man's arm and led him toward the door. The man stumbled, falling against the edge of the table, then wavered a moment before bracing himself against the top of the booth. After getting himself steady, he jerked his arm from the girl's grasp, glaring down on her, then staggered toward the exit alone.

Cole spun back toward his lunch, afraid the girl might say something to him on her way out. Every eye in the diner was on her, and even though it felt like some kind of betrayal, he kept his head down. A moment later, he heard the bell ring on the door and they were gone.

"I hope he ain't driving," Stu said, dumping the glass into the trash can behind the counter.

The whine of the tires on the macadam annoyed Cole as he guided the pickup along the winding road out of Pilot Gap. His turkey sandwich and green beans refused to digest as Thomas talked ceaselessly about night fishing, about where they should go, what time they should head out, how they should dress, crinkling a lake map in his lap, pointing out the coves the tackle store owner had told him to try. Cole took his anger and frustration out the windshield, tried to sink it in the black pavement, in the pine trees and boulders that lined the narrow road, consoling himself with the knowledge he'd only have to endure another twenty minutes of Thomas's blathering before they reached home.

They had just rounded Berry Bend when Cole spotted

smoke alongside the road about a hundred yards ahead. When they got closer, he saw a tan car tangled eerily in the ravine, the passenger side of the car downhill and smashed against a stand of pine trees, the pine trees the only thing keeping the car from tumbling down the steep slope.

Swerving the truck to the edge of the road, Cole dumped the shifter into park, jumped out and ran to the edge of the ravine. A man struggled against the driver-side door, trying to force it open wide enough to crawl out, his knee, shoulder, and head wedged into the stubborn space like a difficult birth. Cole recognized him as the drunk from the diner, the one that had been sitting with Hannah.

Crouching low to the ground, Cole started down the hill, dragging his hand along the dirt for balance, his boots sliding on the mud beneath the layer of dried pine needles. "Wait, Dad. Be careful!" Thomas called to him.

"Try your cell phone, Thomas. Call 911," Cole yelled back, digging his heels into the soil for traction. "Hurry!"

The man seemed exhausted, pushing at the door, the door flopping back against his leg. When Cole got closer, he heard the man swearing, kicking at the door with his other leg, bleeding from his forehead. Cole couldn't see Hannah, couldn't tell if she was okay.

Steam poured from under the hood as Cole forced the door open. The man spilled out onto the ground as if he were made of liquid. Cole helped him to his feet and pointed him up the hill, then ducked his head inside the car to find Hannah. She was slumped against the crushed door, blood at the knee of her jeans.

"What are you doing here?" she said, her eyes bleary, dazed. He leaned in across the seat, easing toward her, the scent of her hair fresh as if she'd just stepped out of the shower. Her wrist fit easily into his palm as he tilted her toward him, placing his other hand on her shoulder.

"Can you scoot toward me?" Cole asked.

"If you get out of my way, I can."

Cole felt foolish as he backed out of the car. With his palms braced against the edge of the roof, he pried the door open with his back and held it while Hannah crawled past the steering wheel. When she was safely out of the car, he twisted himself from the grip of the door and let it slam shut. Hannah stumbled past him, her eyes to the ground. He was about to take her arm, steady her, when something stopped him. He just stood there, watching her, knowing not to help her as she dug her way up the hill.

When Cole reached the road, he saw Thomas hovering over the drunken man who was seated on the gravel shoulder. Cole couldn't speak, couldn't breathe. He bent over and held his knees, gasping for breath, his heart punching at his ribs. He had no idea where Lionel was, or Hannah, his mind trapped in the pattern of stones at his feet. Sprigs of grass pushed up through the parched dirt and gravel. The torn corner of a candy wrapper blew past his toes. For a moment, as he'd struggled down the hill toward the wrecked car, he'd forgotten he was seventy-one, the tight pain in his chest an agonizing reminder.

"She's over here, Grandpa."

Cole twisted his head toward Lionel's voice. Lionel had the passenger-side door of his truck opened, Hannah's feet propped at the bottom edge of the opening. When Cole gathered enough breath to speak, he yelled over at Thomas, asked if the police were coming. Thomas nodded, tending to the man's head. Cole stood up and went over to the truck, to Hannah. Her hands were folded in her lap as if sge were waiting for her name to be called for some kind of award. Blood soaked her jeans at the knee, even though the material wasn't cut.

"What's his name?" Hannah asked Cole, referring to his grandson.

"Lionel."

"What's your name?" Lionel asked Hannah, but Hannah only looked up at Cole—he didn't want this.

"Lionel, go see if your dad needs help," Cole finally said.

"I think he's—"

"Go, Lionel. Wait by the road and wave your hands if cars come by so they slow down. We don't want any more mishaps."

Lionel shuffled away from the truck.

"That was clever," Hannah said. "He's kind of cute. Are you his grandpa?"

The word *grandpa* gave Cole perspective, made him feel old, caused his joints to ache mysteriously, especially given the derisive tone with which she'd said it. He pulled out his pocketknife and clicked it open.

"What do you think you're going to do with that?" Hannah said, leaning away.

"Cut away the leg of your jeans. Check that wound."

"Oh no you're not!" Hannah said, crossing her good leg over the bad one. "These cost thirty-five dollars!"

"We need to look at it."

She held her position for a moment, then leaned forward. "You have a jacket or something?"

Cole reached behind the seat and felt around for his rain poncho. Hannah wrapped it around her waist, draping it down over her legs like a skirt, then reached under and undid her jeans. Cole watched as she wriggled back and forth on the seat, pushing them down.

"Can you give them a little tug?" she asked Cole.

The material of her jeans felt much softer than Cole had imagined, and seemed to have a little give. He'd seen girls in Springfield with skintight jeans and could never figure out how they got in and out of them. Maybe they were stretchy like Hannah's.

It felt inappropriate as he grasped the waist of her jeans, pulling them below her knees, to her ankles. Her skinny belt dangled from the waistband like a dead water snake.

"That's far enough," Hannah said. She raised the poncho to her thighs, so Cole could see the gash. Her shin was covered with blood.

"You're going to need stitches," Cole said, leaning over to get a wad of Hardee's napkins out of his glove box. He grabbed the bottle of water Lionel had bought at the tackle store, wet the napkins, and carefully cleaning the wound. Each time Cole thought he had stopped the bleeding, the wound opened like a faulty seam, releasing more blood. He took the wad of napkins, placed them over the gash, and applied pressure with his right palm, supporting her knee underneath with his left.

"You're loving this, aren't you?" Hannah said. "Touching my leg and all."

Cole was, and felt ashamed that Hannah knew. It wouldn't have been so bad if his intentions had been more nurturing, but the skin beneath her leg was as soft as anything he'd ever felt, like velvet or silk, the two tendons along the bottom of her joint tightening and loosening each time she squirmed in the seat. But more than shame, he was overwhelmed with guilt. He'd already lived his life, handled young legs with a young man's hands, as it should be. Corinne had been sixteen when he'd married her, so he'd had many years of pleasure from tender flesh, years before he knew how precious it was. And he'd forgotten how it felt, the way a man was supposed to forget when it was no longer proper. Yet now, with Hannah's leg between his palms, he was remembering, and couldn't understand why he'd been cursed with such aberrant circuitry, such abominable desires, the remembering bringing nothing but anguish.

Sirens approached from the west, from Mountain View. Cole raised his palm slightly, pulling the napkins up to check the wound.

"They ain't taking me out of this truck with my pants down," Hannah said, the only urgency Cole had ever detected in her voice. "Help me get my jeans up."

"Just a second, Hannah. Wait till they get here."

At that, Hannah's eyes grew wide, concerned, fixed on something beyond Cole's shoulder. Cole hadn't heard Lionel walk up, and, by the look on the boy's face, he'd heard Cole call her Hannah. That wouldn't have mattered much in itself, but it was the tender way Cole had spoken her name that made it too familiar, wrong.

Cole reached behind the seat, grappled through the trash for clean shop towels, wrapping one above Hannah's knee as a tourniquet, the other over the napkins to hold them in place. He turned from Hannah and led Lionel away from the truck so she could dress, then leaned against the front fender, watching his grandson scuff gravel as he walked in the direction of his father.

"Hey, mister," Hannah said to Cole. Cole was glad she hadn't called him by name, even though Lionel was clearly out of earshot. Lionel had already joined his father at the edge of the road, apparently mesmerized by the flashing red and blue lights of the ambulance and sheriff's car as they approached.

"Can you walk?" Cole asked Hannah.

"Yeah . . . thanks."

Cole supported her by the elbow as she slid down off the seat, her good leg coming to rest on the pavement first, the damaged one bent slightly, like a flamingo's.

Hannah looked up at him. "You're coming tonight, aren't you, Cole? You promised, remember?"

Of course he remembered, in the same way he knew it would be impossible to honor his promise. He nodded anyway, a liar's nod, his eyes shifting to the ambulance turning in behind the sheriff's car. The sheriff squatted over the drunken man—who was now stretched out on the pavement as if he'd fallen dead from a heart attack—cradling the man's pulse as two female paramedics rattled a gurney across the road.

"That your father?" Cole asked.

"Don't forget, Cole," she said, hobbling toward the front of his truck. "You promised."

After the paramedics had gotten the man into the ambulance, they seated Hannah in the back next to the gurney. The driver slammed the doors and hurried around to the front, backing the vehicle up before racing away, the siren bleating a second later, the flashing lights pulsing to life.

The sheriff walked to his car, toggled his hand toward Cole before he got in, and sliced a smooth half-circle onto the road to follow the ambulance. Thomas and Lionel strode over, Thomas's palm on Lionel's back, talking in hushed tones reserved for funerals and tragedies, as if speaking too loud might upset the balance of things, tip it the wrong way, pull the misfortune in one's own direction.

Cole squeezed in behind the steering wheel, Lionel

next to him, Thomas at the opposite side, his elbow resting on the edge of the open window. Lionel jostled in the seat a bit, seemingly trying to carve out a little space of his own between his father and grandfather. Cole turned the ignition, resting his foot on the brake as he levered the shift arm to *D*.

"That was the girl from the restaurant, Grandpa," Lionel said. "Did you know her?"

Cole had learned to lie when the truth coiled around him, when it seemed that nothing else would loose the grip. He thought of lies as bursting disks, designed to protect equipment by rupturing under abnormal pressure, form a safe outlet for process fluid—in his life he'd gone through more disks than he wanted to admit.

He'd grown up in Plano, had swallowed his paycheck on many occasions, from barkeepers' bottles in towns he'd never be able to find on a map, had bedded women Corinne would've been sick over, women who laughed and smiled with enough varnish to make even him squirm, but he'd lain with them anyway, their flesh burnished white from the touch of a thousand other men. And he'd lied about all of it at one time or another, bent the truth like a piece of molten steel till it fit the unnatural curve of his life. But he despised himself for lying to his grandson, his own blood pumping through Lionel's veins, as if Lionel's unspoiled heart could purify all the blood and time and truth Cole had tainted.

"She worked at the pharmacy for a spell," Cole said. "At the soda counter." Cole squeezed enough leather against the gas pedal to make the tires yelp when they grabbed the pavement, the hairs on the back of his neck bristling like he'd just robbed a bank. It was a dumb lie and his grandson must have known it. Lionel never said another word the rest of the ride home.

## *Chapter 4*

Lily sat cross-legged, sobbing in the middle of the living room floor, the newspaper at her knees opened to the comics. For a moment, the colorful strips brought to mind travel post-cards, *Greetings from Panama*, *Welcome to Orlando*, *Wish You Were Here*, as if Lily had been planning a wonderful trip. Cole was unsure where the peculiar notion had come from.

Lily's head and shoulders heaved under each new wave of grief, her diamond wedding ring glistening oddly in the fabric of bare fingers covering her face. She seemed intent on crying silently, her upset dying to faint whimpers in her palms, the sound of someone in pain a long way off.

Cole's first thought was Elsie had died. Thomas and Lionel stood inside the doorway, afraid to move, it seemed to Cole, staring at her. Cole knelt down and gently pulled her fingers away. Lily wiped her eyes, then looked back at Thomas and Lionel and forced a stiff smile.

When Cole got Lily seated at the kitchen table, he put the kettle on for tea. Thomas sat next to her, put his hand on hers. She smiled, hugging Lionel to her when he stepped closer.

"I'm sorry," Lily said, sniffling. Thomas motioned for Lionel to get the box of tissues from the coffee table in the living room. "I'm sorry if I worried you. Elsie's okay. She's sleeping."

When Lily settled down enough to talk, she explained what happened, how Elsie started shaking, then fell to the floor, convulsing, her eyes frozen open, saliva bubbling from the corner of her mouth. Lily hadn't known what to do. She'd phoned the doctor, then the hospital in Mountain View, finally the sheriff's office.

"The doctor said she had a grand mal seizure," Lily said. "He gave her an injection of Valium." At this, Lily started crying again, tugging tissues from the box. "It was awful, Daddy. How long has she been this like this? She needs to be in a hospital."

Cole placed a cup of tea in front of Lily, then sat facing her at the table, knowing hospitals were not an option, that Elsie wouldn't allow it. Once they had diagnosed Elsie with a brain tumor, and told her there was not much they could do other than keep her comfortable, Elsie had demanded that Cole take her home. But Elsie had never had seizures before, even though the doctors in Springfield had told him to expect them, that it was only a matter of time.

Lily sipped her tea, then set it down in front of her, staring into the cup as if trying to read something in the amber liquid. She shook her head slowly from side to side, seemingly unaware she was doing it, then looked up, as if snapped from a dream. "Lionel, why don't you go out back. I need to talk to Grandpa."

Cole could tell by the tremor of gravity in Lily's voice that there had been more to the events of the afternoon than she'd already shared, more than the seizure, the visit from the doctor. Lionel walked out onto the deck, sliding the glass door closed behind him.

"I'm going to take Lionel down to the dock," Thomas said, touching Lily's shoulder as he left the kitchen.

"She needs a hospice nurse," Lily said to Cole when they were alone. "The doctor said Aunt Elsie wouldn't go to the hospital, but she needs a nurse. Something."

Cole nodded, remembering his brother-in-law, Herbert, the hospice nurse driving over from Mountain View to take Herbert's blood pressure, his pulse, to talk with him, bringing morphine for the pain. Elsie had called Cole that night, crying, telling him how after the nurse had left, Herbert had called her into the bedroom, held her hand, and said, "I'm dying, aren't I, Elsie? Hospice nurses don't come 'less you're dying, right?" And Elsie hadn't known what to say, even though Herbert had seemed to be accepting the fact, had even told Elsie not to worry, that he wasn't afraid.

"I have friends visit me all the time, talking to me from the other side. I can't see them yet, but I know they're there, Elsie. I hear them." Cole's only experience with death at that point was Corinne's. But Corinne had died suddenly in the kitchen, doctors pinning her death on an aneurysm. Cole was pretty sure Corinne had never heard voices from the other side, or had friends waiting for her in the way Herbert said he had. Even though Cole had not known what to make of Herbert's proclamations, he had felt like Corinne had been cheated out of something by dying so suddenly and unexpectedly, had missed out on some vital assistance in passing over.

Cole phoned the hospice office. Ms. Corbett, who lived in Mountain View, could visit Elsie three times a week. Cole set up an appointment for that evening after dinner so he and Lily could meet her, go over Elsie's history, and also so Ms. Corbett could meet Elsie if she was awake and coherent.

"I think I met Elsie several years ago. I cared for her husband, Herbert," Ms. Corbett told Cole over the phone. "A very dear man."

After Cole hung up, he stood at the back door gazing out over the lake, the unhurried calm of Ms. Corbett's voice circling through his head. Did she know about the voices from the other side, had she heard them while she took care of Herbert, or the hundreds of other people she'd most likely aided on their passage from life to death? The car accident earlier that afternoon came back to Cole, Hannah's father, if it had been her father, sprawled on the side of the road like a dead man. Hannah hadn't seemed concerned, and that had bothered Cole, or maybe it only bothered him now recalling the incident.

"Aunt Elsie said, 'Papa's buried in there.'"

Cole spun from the glass. "What?"

"She pointed toward her bedroom and said, 'Papa's buried in there,'" Lily said. "That's when she started shaking."

Cole had no idea what Lily was talking about. Over the past several weeks Elsie had said things that made no sense, but nothing as strange as that. Lily glared at him, as if for explanation of the odd statement, but Cole had nothing to offer. Maybe she meant Herbert, but he was buried in Mountain View. No, Elsie always called their daddy "Papa." Their daddy had left on numerous occasions when he and Elsie were growing up, and when Cole was fifteen or sixteen—Cole couldn't remember exactly—his daddy left for good. Of course at the time, Cole had no way of knowing he wouldn't return; the idea of him just faded a little with each pink sunrise till his daddy ceased being a thought at all.

Cole was fairly certain his father had to be gone from the world by now, but had no idea where he might have been buried, if indeed he ever had been. Whenever Cole imagined him dead, he always pictured him in an alley somewhere in Houston, stabbed to death, or shot through the chest, left to waste away naturally, absorbed back into the earth like a rotting screwbean mesquite or pile of manure. Cole had never been able to picture him all suited-up, nestled into some satin-lined mahogany casket like a fancy chocolate in a Whitman's Sampler box. His daddy never would have stood for that, not even in his death.

"Aunt Elsie said something else I didn't understand," Lily added. "Something about a spitfire."

Lily seemed much more at ease after Ms. Corbett left the house, Cole thought, backing his bass boat from the slip. He had been relieved as well by Ms. Corbett's buoyant attitude, her graceful approach to death and dying, explaining calmly which medicines to administer at what times. "And you have my phone number," she had assured both of them. Cole had hoped Elsie would wake and remember Ms. Corbett, but she'd slept through the entire visit.

"Sit here," Cole told Lionel, patting the compartment lid between himself and Thomas. Thomas slid his arm over the boy's shoulder, twisting Lionel's cap around so it wouldn't blow off during the boat ride. It bothered Cole when Thomas did that, as if Thomas should have found the boy a cap that fit properly. Everything Thomas did seemed to irritate Cole, right down to his unflagging enthusiasm.

Cole had decided earlier that afternoon to take Thomas and Lionel to Miller Creek, where the banks were steep, cut from sheer granite, plummeting sharply into seventy feet of water. Not much chance of catching shallow spinnerbait fish there and not one speck of pea gravel for miles. The idea was that Thomas and Lionel would get bored punching holes in the sterile water and want to go in after an hour or so. Cole had already pictured the scene, driving them back up the lake, Lionel sleepy-eyed and Thomas frustrated, letting them out on the dock, telling them that he wanted to try a few more spots before coming in. Then he'd swing the boat around and head to Turnback Creek, keep his promise to Hannah, but more than that, satisfy his own longing. But that's where the crystal ball clouded. What was he hoping for? Cole never pictured himself actually holding Hannah's body next to his, or kissing her in any romantic way, yet he wanted to be with her, wanted something he couldn't define, or was afraid to, and even worse, he felt he would get it eventually, whatever it was.

Cole stopped the boat within thirty feet of the long granite bluff in Miller Creek. In the dying blue of twilight, the rock face stood before them like a prison wall. Bracing himself against protests, Cole hurried to the bow of the boat, picked up his rod, and tossed his spinnerbait to where the stone face disappeared beneath the water. Hoping to suppress any doubts Thomas might have, Cole felt he had to show great conviction in the spot, to fish confidently and intently, even though he was fairly certain they wouldn't catch a thing. And they didn't. For over an hour and a half.

"Cole, I don't think this is the right kind of bank," Thomas said, obviously trying to extend Cole respect, while at the same time questioning his choice of fishing spots. "The guy at the tackle store told me, 'gently sloping pea gravel banks.' Maybe we could try one of those."

Cole was troubled by the suggestion, hoping Thomas would have thrown in the towel by now and asked to be taken back to the house. After all, the plan had been working—Lionel had grown bored and weary and fallen asleep on the floor, while Thomas had seemed to be losing interest, looking up at the stars frequently, and stopping to eat red licorice instead of fishing. Cole had been thinking that at any moment Thomas would lay his rod down in defeat.

"He showed me several places on the map," Thomas said.

Cole heard the crinkling sound of stiff paper being unfurled, could see in his mind the map spread out in Thomas's lap, a tiny flashlight held between his teeth.

"He circled a spot called Cow Pen Cove, and another called Pine Branch," Thomas said. "Are we close to those?"

Cow Pen Cove was only a few minutes' ride from Miller Creek. Cole had caught plenty of fish in there in spring, and Thomas was right: Cow Pen had the perfect pea-gravel banks, which was why Cole was so upset when Thomas hooked a bass on his first cast in Cow Pen. No sooner had Thomas landed the nice three-pounder than Lionel found his rod and started casting toward shore. Cole hooked the next fish and knew there'd be no way to get Thomas and Lionel off the lake now.

They caught and released numerous bass over the next two hours. When it slowed, Cole announced another spot that should be just as good. "Let's head up to Turnback Creek," Cole said. He believed they'd catch fish in Turnback, and probably big ones, but more than that, Hannah would see with her own eyes why he hadn't been able to keep his promise, provided she was still waiting for him by the lake. He pictured her sitting on the bank, smoking a cigarette, her knees folded up to her chest, hair clipped or pinned back—he couldn't tell—like some queer plant growing from her scalp. Hannah radiated a resilient impermanence Cole had never seen in any child before, like the graceful tenacity of a bull rider lashed to a sixteen-hundred-pound brindle—flowing with the pump and thrust of the beast's fierce muscle one second, gored to death the next. Cole had witnessed such an incident in Laramie and never forgot it, and even though the cowboy lacked the celebrity of Lane Frost, his death was no less horrifying. Hannah seemed to have the same tragic ease about her, as if she were bound to some untamable creature, one that terrified and spirited her.

Turnback was less than a ten-minute ride from Miller Creek, a much shorter distance than Cole had remembered. He had wanted more time to think, decide whether or not this was a good idea. What if Hannah came strolling down the bank wearing shorts, smoking her cigarette—the bandage covering her newly stitched knee shining like a no-trespassing sign in the night—and called his name? Worse yet, what if she came down naked carrying her pistol? Maybe he could fish the far bank, but then how would she see he was there, how would she know that Thomas and Lionel had been the reason he'd been unable to fulfill his promise? But more than that, why did he care? Hannah was no one to him. She wasn't kin—he hardly knew her. He owed her nothing. He had no reason to provide any excuse for falling back on his word. He was, after all, seventy-one years old, far beyond intrigue, or propitiating a teenager. But Hannah had erased some part of him, as if the tally of his years, and all the experiences along the way, no longer mattered, no longer provided substance or clout. He was reduced to awe, the way any man, no matter his age, would stand petrified at the crumbling edge of a bottomless canyon.

Cole eased along the bank until he saw the thresher. Without a word, he shut off the motor, picked up his rod, and started casting. Lionel stood in the center walkway and Thomas sat in the back pedestal seat, both of them throwing their spinnerbaits toward the bank, sometimes landing them on it, the metal blades tinkling against the rocks.

They had only fished about thirty yards when a loud splash split the night. At first, Cole figured Thomas had hooked a huge fish and hadn't said anything, which was unlike him—he always announced a fish the second he'd hung one. Lionel's rod stood straight out from the edge of the boat, his spinnerbait dangling off the end.

"Wow, Grandpa. That sounded like a big fish." Lionel leaned forward over the edge, watching the same ripples off the bow of the boat Cole was looking at. Cole thought maybe it had been a carp, but he'd never seen or heard one jump at night. When the second splash exploded ten feet behind the boat, Lionel's head snapped around, Cole's following, their eyes on the rip in the water.

"Jeez, Dad," Thomas said to Cole, "do fish always jump like that at night?"

That was no fish, Cole thought, fairly certain he knew what it was. Maybe Hannah wasn't good with a pistol, but she had quite an arm for chunking rocks, the lump on the back of his head proof of that. He let his eyes rove the jagged edge of woods, survey the shore, expecting to spot her crouched behind a rock. But she wasn't—she stood out in the open about twenty feet from the water, her arms loose at her sides, as though she were waiting for a cab. She stared directly at Cole, yet Thomas and Lionel didn't seem to notice her, their attention on the splash.

"Let's fish the far bank," Cole said, jumping down from the deck and firing the motor. He had already spun the boat away from Hannah before Thomas could get down from the rear seat. "Those are carp jumping. Bass don't bite around carp." Cole had stated the lie with such authority that it seemed true even to his own ears. Idling across the creek, Cole glanced back over his shoulder, hoping Hannah had left, and was surprised to see her still standing there, like a piece of driftwood on the shore, her silhouette slowly merging into the black backdrop of trees.

## *Chapter 5*

Lily was on her hands and knees scrubbing the kitchen floor when they walked in. Cole looked up at the clock—two-thirty in the morning. Thomas hurried past him to the bathroom, saying a quick hello to Lily, while Lionel rummaged the refrigerator.

"Mom, is there anything to eat?"

When Lily shot him a scornful look, he shuffled away with a handful of grapes.

"What are you doing, Lily?" Cole asked. "What happened?"

Lily shook her head, then looked over at Lionel, then back to the floor. Cole knew she didn't like talking about Elsie in front of Lionel.

"Lionel, why don't you turn the television on real quiet?" Cole said.

"I'm going to bed as soon as Dad gets out of the bathroom. That was really fun, Grandpa. I've never caught so many fish. And I had the biggest, right?"

Cole nodded. Lily looked up and said, "How big was your fish, Lionel?"

"Five pounds, right, Grandpa?"

"Yep. Quite a fish," Cole said. Lily smiled and held her arms out to Lionel. He broke from her hug when Thomas came into the kitchen. "Good night everybody," Lionel said, throwing his grape stems in the trash as he left the room.

When Lily took the soapy bucket to the kitchen sink, Cole sat himself at the table. Thomas sat across from him.

"You know what she was doing when I got up?" Lily said, her hand on her hip, a wisp of hair falling down her forehead. "Cooking. Melting chocolate chips in a saucepan, then crushing potato chips in her hands and dumping them in the chocolate. She said it was topping for her ice cream, which was melting on the table and dripping onto the floor. She talked, but not to me. It was like I wasn't even here."

Cole recalled the night Elsie mixed corn flakes with whipped cream and peanut butter and ate it from a ladle. The doctor had told him that the Sombien could have that possible side effect, that people would sleepwalk to the kitchen and eat fatty, high-caloric foods, then wake up with no memory of it the next morning. The doctor had told him not to worry, that no one had ever hurt themselves. But this was new. Elsie had never used the stove before, and that worried Cole. "Did she turn the burner off?" Cole asked.

"Are you kidding? She didn't even put the ice cream back in the freezer. The chocolate in the pan was burnt to a crisp. There were potato chip crumbs all over the floor. Christ, Daddy, she could have burned the damn house down."

Cole didn't think it was that serious—after all, the stove was electric. Back in Oklahoma he'd come home tired from a long night of working and drinking and was reheating chili when he'd fallen asleep on the living room sofa. The next morning the pot was melted down the front of the gas stove, the flame still burning. Surprisingly nothing had caught fire. He figured electric had to be a bit safer than gas.

"That's not all, Daddy," Lily said. "She told me she would be the British, that I should take the hellcat. Then she went to bed."

Cole had forgotten all about the Spitfire and Hellcat. When he and Elsie were kids, Cole had made two rope swings in the barn out of old tires he'd found. He had climbed up in the hayloft to secure the ropes to the main beam, spacing the swings wide enough apart that they could trace large circles without hitting each other. Occasionally they would hit anyway, but that was half the fun, trying to dodge each other. He and Elsie would get in the swings and kick off with their feet, pretending to be fighter pilots in a World War II dogfight. Elsie always wanted to be the British, fly the Spitfire. Cole didn't care. Elsie had a better British accent because her teacher at school had been from England, and Elsie had copied her dialect perfectly. Sometimes he'd be the Japanese or Germans fighting against Elsie, but mostly he'd play the Americans and they would fight side-by-side against an invisible enemy, reenacting machine gun fire noises and plane crash explosions. Cole was better at those. He'd even painted the blue and red British target emblem on the tread of Elsie's tire.

They'd had fun playing together in the barn until one day Elsie refused to go in there anymore, refused to feed the horses or clean out the stalls. Cole had to do all the barn chores by himself after that. He'd even complained to his mother once and she had told him that Elsie was turning into a young lady and shouldn't be doing chores of that kind any longer, that it wouldn't kill him to take care of the horses, that Elsie would help with dishes, laundry, and cooking, that that's what Elsie needed to be learning anyhow. When it was time to put up the hay, it was Cole's mother, not Elsie, who came out to help him.

That was after their father had left. His mother took a job in a law office in town, Gore and Spivey, and made good money as a secretary. Even though Cole couldn't work the farm by himself after that, neighbors helped out to bring in the crops until Cole joined the Navy. A year later, his mother sold the horses, then the farm, and bought a small house on the edge of town. She never remarried.

"Daddy, you okay?" Lily asked.

Cole looked up, surprised to see Lily standing there, still feeling the pull of the memory. He nodded. Lily kissed him on the head before she and Thomas went to bed. Cole sat alone in the kitchen, listening to the refrigerator, thinking about Elsie, then about Hannah, about hearing the backhoe loader rumbling through the woods. The noise had started soon after they had crossed Turnback Creek to fish the other side, away from Hannah. Even though Turnback was only a couple hundred yards wide, the cove was so long it would have taken Hannah over three hours to walk around to the far bank, if she could have walked around at all. He couldn't get her silhouette out of his mind, her pose of dejection, shoulders slumped, arms limp at her sides. Maybe she'd been crying—it had been impossible to see her face.

For the next two days it stormed, making it impossible for Cole to fish at night. The first night, Cole was relieved for the excuse not to go up to Turnback Creek and see Hannah, ready to be done with the strange affair. But the following afternoon, when Thomas and Lionel drove back to Kansas City, leaving Cole alone to go out at night, his intrigue was reignited.

Elsie was getting worse and didn't seem to know anyone, sleeping most of the time, refusing to eat when she was awake. The hospice nurse had made a special trip during the storm after Elsie suffered another seizure.

Lily had decided not to go back to Kansas City so she could help with Elsie, even though Cole had insisted she go, assuring her that he and Elsie would be just fine. But Lily refused to leave, and had called work, telling them she needed off till the following weekend.

"Do you think you should have done that?" Cole asked. "You shouldn't miss work."

"I've got lots of sick days. Besides, I don't think Elsie . . . I want to be here."

Lightning strikes over the lake were spectacular. He and Lily sat at the kitchen table not speaking, her reading the paper, sipping coffee, him watching the rich blackness outside the windows, listening to the rain hiss along the deck boards. During the brilliant flashes of lightning, Cole caught the peculiar slant of the rain, saw the branches on Elsie's cedar trees flail in the gusts as if at any moment the limbs could be ripped free, as if they were losing the bid for their survival. Cole knew the cedar roots behind Elsie's house couldn't burrow any deeper than a foot or so before hitting solid granite, then had to spread through the ground along the buried rock, seeking out cracks and breaches to grab hold of. It was hard to imagine how they could hold a trunk firm under such a thrashing.

Lily made no move toward the storm, never looked up from her newspaper, even when thunder rattled the glasses in Elsie's sideboard. At first Cole had thought nothing of Lily's silence. It was the kind they'd shared for years out of respect, he'd always thought, for their mutual disdain for small talk and empty conversation. But this quiet was different somehow, had a restrained urgency about it that left a huge hole in the room, one that was hard to ignore.

"I'm glad you stayed," Cole said.

"I stayed for Elsie."

"Yes, I know. But I appreciate—"

"Why do you leave Elsie alone every night?" Lily folded the newspaper in front of her and stared at him.

"I only leave after she falls asleep. It gives me time to—"

"You should be here. All the time."

Cole didn't like the tone Lily had taken with him. He was about to rebuke her but instead got up to go to bed, too tired and weary in the moment to fight.

"I'll see you in the morning," he said, touching her shoulder as he walked past.

"Why were you never with Mama?" Lily said. "Why did you always leave her alone?"

"I traveled with the work. You know that."

"I'm not talking about when you traveled. I'm talking about when you were home. When you were home you were never home."

Cole shook his head. It was all too long ago, and too tiring to work at remembering. Life didn't lay itself out in neat little chapters that you could go back and reread like a novel. Life happened as it happened, with its own reasons, its own purposes, causes of events and choices that may never be understood or recalled, motives that may never reveal themselves. And what was the point anyway? What could it change? He wasn't about to defend himself against the past, a past that would neither mold itself to convenient ideals, nor change to suit the needs of the present.

No, he was not going to look back, not tonight, not at seventy-one years old, not ever. Cole took a step toward the bathroom, feeling his chin, thinking he might need a shave before he went to bed.

"Mama knew you cheated on her. Did you know that?"

Cole stopped, unable to face Lily. He took another step toward the bathroom and heard Lily's chair scuff across the floor, could feel her moving toward him, the floor creaking under her approach. Soon she was in front of him, her eyes in his. Everyone had always said Lily looked like him more than her mother. Cole had never been able to see it, especially now. Lily's eyes were red, the skin across her chin tightened till it shone like polished marble. She was beautiful, like Corinne, but didn't remind him of her at all. Where Corinne was fair, Lily was dark, her hair black, dyed, Cole thought, and her eyes green. Corinne's face had been an oval platter, while Lily's was shaped more like a shovel, sharp at the chin, wide and exotic at the forehead.

"She knew, Daddy. She'd wait up till she heard you coming in, then she'd rush off to bed, pretend to be asleep."

Lily's teeth flashed white and straight and Cole remembered taking her for braces. As a child, Cole's teeth had been bad, like his father's. But Corinne's teeth had always been striking. It was one of the first things that had attracted him to her—anyone with such fine teeth, he'd reasoned, had to be a good person. Corinne had assured him Lily's teeth would be beautiful as well, but Cole was never sure braces alone would do the trick. Anytime he was in town, he made a dentist appointment for her, then waited for her in the truck, reading a magazine. He hated doctors' offices.

"You know what I told her, Daddy?"

Cole tried to walk past Lily but she grabbed his arm.

"I told her she should get rid of you, Daddy," she said. "I told her she should throw you out."

Cole had always felt it some form of punishment for him the way Corinne had died so suddenly, denying him any chance to tell her things that he'd already put off for far too long. The night she died, they had finished dinner and planned on going to a movie after the table was cleared and the garbage taken out. While Corinne had rinsed dishes in the sink, Cole had pulled the plastic bag from the trash can and carried it out to the metal can at the side of the house. When he'd come back in, Corinne was lying on the kitchen floor. At first, thinking she'd fallen and been knocked unconscious, he'd knelt down next to her, trying to revive her. That's when he'd noticed the blue coloring in her lips. He'd felt for a pulse but got nothing. After ripping open her blouse, he fumbled with her bra, trying to get it free. Unable to reach the clasp beneath her back, he took out his pocketknife and cut it in the front so her chest would be unrestricted. He reached his finger into her mouth to clear her breathing passage, then pinched her nostrils shut, covering her mouth with his. He breathed into her lungs, expanding her chest over and over without response before jumping up for the phone and dialing 911. When he returned to Corinne, he tried pumping her lungs with the palms of his hands, and for a moment she seemed to respond, color coming into her lips, flushing pink, but the doctor explained later that there was nothing he could have done, that her lips had only colored because of the blood he'd forced through her veins.

With the image of Corinne fading inside his memory, Cole looked over at Lily, her eyes wet and red. "You told her the right thing, Lily," Cole said. "She should have listened to you."

When Cole walked past Elsie's bedroom, he heard her moaning. He stopped at the door, listening, his mind with Lily's statement, how she'd told Corinne to get rid of him. It was hard to imagine how Lily had known of his affairs, or that she'd had such strong feelings about them. He wondered how Corinne must have felt, how she'd known—she had never let on about anything.

Elsie moaned again and Cole opened the door slowly so as not to startle her, but she was already out of bed, standing in the corner, shaking her head and repeating something Cole couldn't understand. He held her by the shoulders and guided her back to bed. Lily stood in the doorway and Cole wondered if she had more to say to him.

He didn't really want to hear any more, wanted nothing to do with the past. He pulled the blanket up around Elsie's shoulders and she mumbled something to Cole as he stepped away from the bed. He was fairly certain Elsie was not fully conscious, but he asked her to repeat what she'd said.

"Don't put Candy Bar in her stall, Cole. Don't ever put her back in that stall." Elsie grabbed his wrist and wouldn't let go. Cole was surprised by her grip—Elsie had lacked the strength to lift a spoonful of oatmeal over the past couple days.

"Candy Bar shouldn't be in there anymore," she said, her eyes closed, her fingers uncoiling from his wrist.

He recalled how Candy Bar had bucked and protested going into her stall that afternoon he'd come home from school. Elsie had been upset about something that day. Candy Bar was grazing in the field and Elsie would have been the one to put her horse away, but his mother had insisted Cole should get Candy Bar and put fresh straw in her stall. But when he started to lead her in, the horse reared and whinnied, backing up on its hind legs across the barn. She had never acted like that before. It was then he'd noticed Elsie standing in the entrance to the barn, sobbing, shaking. "Come help me," Cole had said, and Elsie ran back to the house. Cole had never been able to coax the horse back into the stall.

After Cole helped Elsie back into bed, he closed the door slowly and was about to go to the bathroom when Lily touched his arm. "Daddy, I'm sorry about what I said."

"You have no reason to be sorry, Lily." Cole wanted to say more, say all the things that never seemed to get said, offer all the apologies that were far too late in coming, provide all the explanations that seemed inadequate in explaining anything. "We're all tired, Lily. Let's just go to bed."

Lily stood in the doorway of the spare bedroom a moment. "I'm sorry about Elsie, Daddy."

Cole nodded, shutting the bathroom door behind him. He appreciated Lily's help, but having her around was taxing. He knew she harbored a repressed anger toward him, one that had begun to harden but could still erupt without warning. And unless she was speaking to Lionel or hugging Thomas, her eyes were always glossed with resentment, or indolent with sadness. He pictured her content most of the time, at least when she was home in Kansas City, and he was thankful for her happiness, even if it was contingent on not being around him. He figured his presence must be taxing for her as well.

After he finished in the bathroom, he lay a long time in bed, listening to the furnace cycle on and off, the air rushing through the vents. The storm seemed to have passed, and Cole pulled back the curtains to see the long shadows the moonlight drew across the yard. The wet grass glistened as if covered in light frost, making it appear colder than it was. For the first time all day he thought about Hannah, how she'd looked a few nights ago standing shadow still on the shore. Would she be angry with him too? Would he see the same seasoned disappointment in Hannah's eyes that was always present in Lily's? Had it been in Corinne's? He tried to remember.

# *Chapter 6*

The night air had a thin, refreshing chill that Cole had come to love. Unable to sleep, he had dressed and crept from the house, down to the dock, deciding to fish for a few hours, thinking about Hannah. The dock rocked and creaked as he walked toward his boat, the sound and movement making the dark world around him tangible. The wet-wood smell of the boards brought to mind the odor of bedding straw in Candy Bar's stall. Cole had never given much thought to the horse's resistance that day, or Elsie's refusal to go in the barn and care for the horse. He'd always figured a rattler had gotten in there and scared Candy Bar. She was a bit skittish to begin with, afraid to cross a stream even if it was only two inches deep. There had been a locust tree near the fence that, over the years, had grown into the barbed wire, the wire encased in the trunk as if it had been carefully threaded through. Cole had always been bewildered by the wire passing through the trunk and had ridden Candy Bar out there one day. They had encountered a timber rattler at the base of the fence and Candy Bar, so frightened by the hissing and rattling, had bolted and would never go near that tree again.

Cole started the outboard motor, the clatter of pistons echoing off the tin roof of the dock. He recalled coming home from school that day, how the clouds painted large buffalo shadows across the fields, like a herd passing through. He had stood out at the fence a long time watching, his books on the ground, letting the cool air of autumn wash across his face. Candy Bar grazed in the distance, dwarfed beneath the immense white clouds. When he'd walked to the house, he'd stopped on the front porch listening to sobbing from the upstairs window and knew it was Elsie. Elsie had stayed home sick that day, complaining of a bellyache and other ailments Cole had been sure she was faking. That was also the day his father had left, the way he had on several other occasions. At the time Cole didn't know that his father would never write or call.

Backing out of the slip, Cole swung the boat toward the main lake, toward Turnback Creek. He wasn't sure if Hannah would be there, but he'd already decided to find her if she wasn't. He needed to see her.

Cole's father had been drunk that morning when Cole left for school. Cole's father had been sitting at the kitchen table, telling Elsie she needed to eat breakfast, pushing the plate of bacon and toast across the table toward her. But Elsie refused to eat, grabbing her belly and grimacing. Cole's father laughed and said a young healthy girl like her shouldn't be suffering from bellyaches, then poured her a glass of milk and told her to drink it. Elsie pleaded, saying that she would throw up if she had to drink it, but his father just laughed again, saying how dramatic she was. "Well, if you're going to stay home from school, then you need to help with the chores," his father had said. "Lot of work to be done in the barn." At that, Elsie started to cry. Cole's mother spun toward his father and told him Elsie was too sick to work in the barn, or she'd be going to school. "She looks just fine to me," his father had said. "What is it, Elsie, a boy at school you don't want to see?" His father laughed again, then took a piece of bacon from her plate and pushed it into his mouth. Cole remembered staring at his father and his father noticing. "What are you looking at? You need to get on to school, boy, unless you have a bellyache too." "Yes sir," Cole had said, grabbing his books off the chair on his way out the door. "Wait, Cole," his mother called, hugging him, her eyes beginning to wet. She whispered to him, "I'm sorry." He never understood why she'd said that. She wiped her eyes then dried her hands on her apron and helped Elsie out of the chair. "Come on, sweetie, let's put you to bed."

Cole was leaping down the steps when he heard his father yelling at his mother, then laughing, then yelling. His father laughed a lot when he was drunk—it was the only time he laughed. But Cole never felt that he laughed because he was happy, not like his mother. She had laughed when a storm moved in and tore the laundry line loose from the pole, carrying the sheets like ship sails across the field. They had all started running ater the sheets, Cole, his mother and Elsie, howling with laughter, trying to rein them in. She laughed when she read *Huck Finn* and *Tom Sawyer* to them in the evenings, creating different voices for each of the characters. She laughed when the transmission went out on the way to town and Mr. Halpern gave them a ride in the back of his pickup truck and it poured rain. Cole recalled her laugh more than anything else about her.

He guided his boat into Turnback Creek, the hull skimming smooth as polish across the flat lake. The waning moon was a lopsided dish above the black cut of trees, throwing light across the rocky banks, causing them to glow like snow-dusted fields against the colorless dark water. In Plano, where Cole had walked the low hills as a kid, snow was a rarity. But when it came, it arrived like sifted flour on the rocks and ruts, bleaching the brown Texas landscape white. Like a mirage, the snow would melt within a few days and seldom fell in enough quantity to make a snowman, but Cole loved to find the tracks of bobtail cats and track them to where they hunted and lived.

Cole noticed a ripple on the water as he slowed the boat, watching for the thresher on the bank, training his eyes along the shore looking for Hannah. It was late, maybe too late for her to be out, but like him, she seemed to need little sleep. When he'd left the house, he was determined to find her and tell her he wouldn't be coming back, that he'd do what he promised but that was it. She would never see him again. That decision conversely both soothed and distressed him. Wanting Hannah, whether he acted on his yearning or not—and he was fairly sure he wouldn't—was wrong.

After tying off the boat, Cole stepped onto the shore, rocks shifting and crunching beneath his boots. The air was frail and thin, as if incapable of supporting sound. Even the stars seemed fragile, frozen crystals that might evaporate at any moment.

The canopy of leaves grew thick, squeezing the moonlight into pale streaks and blotches on the forest floor. Cole switched on his flashlight and hoped to hear the backhoe loader, some sign that Hannah was up and around even though it was nearly four in the morning.

The two-story house belonging to Hannah's grandmother seemed out of place rising from the wide, weedy clearing, as if a helicopter had plopped the dwelling down in the only suitable spot on the property. Cole saw the backhoe loader sitting idle in the yard next to the rectangular patch of red clay that had been dug out and scraped level for a concrete foundation. He wondered why Hannah's grandmother was building a new house, if she planned to raze the old one, which seemed to be in decent condition. Maybe Hannah and her father would live in the new house. Cole wondered if her father was there now, or if he was still in the hospital. But her father hadn't seemed to be hurt badly, and hospitals tended to release folks as soon as they were able to get to the bathroom by themselves. The thought of her father being at home made him reluctant to go any closer. How would Cole explain his presence? And would he have a chance to? Maybe Hannah's father carried a pistol around like Hannah. And maybe he was a better shot.

The house was dark and seemingly void of life. Cole stepped from the bracken and felt like he'd stepped onto a stage, the moonlight suddenly bright on his face. Cole thought about Hannah's drunken father, wondered if he was dangerous, but he didn't care. Cole thought about testing fate, dying such a bizarre and reprehensible death—shot while sneaking in the middle of the night to see a fourteen-year-old girl. Cole had once read about Crow warriors who were called Crazy Dogs Wanting to Die. Crazy Dogs were believed to be either insane or so saddened by life they charged into battle, hoping to be killed by their enemy. Cole had never felt that he wanted to die, but at times, he'd not really cared about living, and wondered if that's what made Crazy Dogs such ruthless warriors. He wasn't feeling ruthless, or warrior-like, but something inside him didn't care anymore, as if standing in the safety of darkness was a less desirable option than being crushed in the light.

Dry twigs from the previous summer crackled underfoot as he strode across the field toward the dark shape of the house. Even though he felt some sort of release from fear, he conjured excuses in his head just the same—some reason for his being there if Hannah's father suddenly appeared on the front porch—but came up with nothing suitable. Maybe he'd just tell him that he'd promised Hannah he would show her how to operate the bucket on the backhoe loader. That's what Hannah had wanted. She could never get it to work right, could never get it to dig a hole. Cole had asked her what she needed a hole for, and she had smiled and said, "Because." Cole hadn't pursued a reason, figuring she was bored with the night, but needed to fill it with something, new lest morning arrive as a disheartening repeat of the previous day. The only thing that carried Cole through some days with Elsie was the memory of the night before, a bass that fought particularly hard, or the sweet smell of honeysuckle drifting across a dark, flat cove. Sometimes it was just recalling the pure simplicity of night, the gentle rhythm of water purling against the hull, or a raccoon sticking his paws under rocks along the bank foraging crawfish, crunching the crustaceans between its teeth. He had once watched a raccoon for almost an hour, the raccoon hunting without concern for Cole's presence.

When Cole drew within fifty feet of the house, Hannah walked out onto the porch in baggy white pajamas, as if she'd been waiting on him, and leaned against the rail. It felt queer and intoxicating, yet natural, as if Cole should be returning home from the road, a young wife waiting for him. Corinne had looked no older than Hannah when they'd married.

"Where you been?" Hannah asked before he reached the porch. "What do you want? You shouldn't be here, an old man like you. It's creepy. You know that, don't you?"

"How's your knee?" Cole asked.

"Fine. Want to see?" At that, Hannah raised her pant leg, exposing her calf and the stitches above her knee.

"Why are you still up?"

Hannah sat on the steps and lit a cigarette. "Couldn't sleep. The storm was too loud, so I came out here and watched it. It was like some kind of sci-fi movie when it ended. This big cloud filled with lightning just moved across the sky and the rain and wind stopped and the moon came out. It was kind of spooky."

"I can't stay," said Cole. "I'll show you how to work that scoop like I promised, if you want me to, then I need to get going. My sister's dying." Cole wasn't sure why he'd added the part about Elsie. Maybe if Hannah knew he was facing the death of a loved one, he wouldn't seem so pitiful.

"I don't have any brothers or sisters." Hannah stood, then turned to go in the house. "I'll put on some jeans." When Hannah returned, she continued talking as if she hadn't left. "But I have a best friend who's just like a sister. Her name is Amy." Hannah buttoned her jeans as she bounded down the steps. "Her dad is a photographer in Anchorage and he has this cool cabin. Have you ever heard of Talkeetna?"

Cole shook his head and smelled apricots as Hannah walked by him.

"Well, he has this cabin in Talkeetna and Amy and I are going up there with him this summer to help him and stuff. He's even going to pay me. I don't know how much, though, but I can't imagine the work will be hard. Amy says all we have to do is get him stuff, like lenses and things, and help him carry his equipment into the woods. He's a wildlife photographer. He even has a book of his work, one of those big ones that weighs about a ton."

Hannah jumped up on the backhoe loader like she'd been driving one all her life. "Won't this wake your dad?" Cole asked, as she was about to turn the key.

"He's not here," she said, and the loader coughed to life, the pistons slapping, metal against metal, until the exhaust pipe kicked out a big swarm of blue smoke into the night sky. The image of Hannah sitting tall in the seat, hands clasped to the wheel, reminded Cole of Elsie. Elsie had been nine when she'd begged Cole to let her drive the tractor. "Please, Cole, let me drive it once. I can do it." Cole had looked down from the seat and known he shouldn't, but who would find out anyway? He jumped down from the tractor and helped Elsie up into the seat. "Scoot forward so you can reach the pedals," he'd told her. Her fingers had looked so frail and thin wrapped around the steering wheel. "Now what?" she asked, eyes bright and round as bottle caps. Cole had shown her how to operate the pedals, then stood on the hitch holding onto the back of the seat. Elsie howled when the tractor starting moving. She was a small silhouette against the horizon, the tractor jouncing her back and forth in the huge seat. Elsie hadn't driven the tractor more than fifty yards when Cole felt a hand on his shirt, pulling him from the tractor, throwing him to the ground. His father screamed for Elsie to stop, then leapt up onto the tractor and turned off the key. "What the hell were you thinking about letting her drive the tractor?" Cole's father shouted, slapping him across the back of the head. He pulled Elsie off the tractor seat. "She's just a child. Get this field done and quit fooling around." Cole picked up his cap and watched his father drag Elsie by the hand across the field, leading her toward the barn, yelling that if she wanted to help with things, there were plenty of chores in the barn. He didn't see Elsie again until supper. Elsie didn't eat or say a thing through the entire meal, then went to bed.

Hannah shouted over the rumble of the diesel engine. "Are you going to show me how to work this thing or not?"

"This here's a parallel-lift loader, which means you can hold more dirt in the bucket than a regular loader," Cole told her, his attention split between Hannah and the memory of Elsie.

"I don't care about any of that. I just want to dig a hole."

He explained the two joysticks, that the left one moved the boom and backhoe from side to side, and that the right one worked the bucket. "That's your main control. You'll use it the most. Push it to the left, the bucket scoops in. Push to the right, it dumps." He instructed her to pull it toward her to raise the arm, then away to lower it.

Hannah squealed. "This is fun!"

"You have to learn to work the right and left stick together."

Hannah lowered the bucket and managed to scrape the grass from the ground.

"You have to push it away, then to the left," Cole told her.

After several more attempts, Hannah gouged out a respectable chunk of earth, lifting it toward the sky. "Now what?"

"Push the left stick to the right, then the right one to the right."

The bucket dumped the dirt back in the hole. "You have to move the left one first, to swing the boom, then the right one."

"You said the right one was the important one," said Hannah, obviously frustrated, glaring down at Cole.

"Let me show you." Cole climbed up into the loader. Hannah scooted over and watched him from beside the seat. Cole toggled the joysticks and quickly scooped out a bucket full of dirt and dropped it several feet to the side of the hole. "Like that."

Hannah practiced for several minutes, while Cole wedged in behind her. With Hannah's back resting against him, he felt each movement of her arms as she operated the joysticks. Occasionally the scent of apricots would break through the oily stench of burnt diesel, and he caught himself leaning forward, closer to her hair. Her shoulders seemed wide but not very thick, like the top edge of a two-by-four.

"Where's your father?" Cole asked.

"He stays in town with his girlfriend. I can't stand her. She never shuts up."

"You probably shouldn't be digging here where they're going to build."

"Max, he's the contractor, told me this is where they're putting the septic tank."

Cole watched over Hannah's shoulder as she pushed the bucket into the earth, the cylinders whirring as she levered the sticks. She was doing better than most rookies, even though her excavation was becoming a ragged mess, none of the edges straight or clean. The hole was approximately four feet deep and ten feet long before she switched off the ignition. "That's enough for tonight." She hopped down from the loader and started walking toward the house, not waiting for Cole. Cole eased himself down from the cab, then arched backward, trying to relieve the kink in his spine. It had been years since he'd operated equipment. When he was younger, he'd been able to sit for hours running a loader or bulldozer.

A moment later Hannah appeared with two cans of beer, pushing one into Cole's palm. He hadn't had a beer in over twelve years, not since his DUI and his promise to Corinne.

"You could bury a man where no one would ever find him," Hannah said.

"What?"

"You could bury a man there, where they're going to put the concrete foundation, and no one would ever find him once the house was built."

Cole looked over at the dirt, the moon coloring it a deep burgundy. He supposed you could, but still thought it an odd thing to say. He figured you could bury a man out in the middle of a field and most likely no one would find him either, or at the bottom of Hardman Lake, or a thousand other places, for that matter. That didn't seem to be the point, how to hide a dead body. The real question was why would you need to hide the body in the first place, unless you'd killed him? Cole pictured Hannah's father slumped in the booth at Stu's diner, and her scraping her fork across the waffles, ignoring her father. He hadn't even bothered looking for her at the bottom of the ravine, just scrabbled out of the car, trying to get up the hill. Cole would have looked for Lily if it had been him driving, would have tried to pull her free, make sure she was all right.

"I spent a year at Mercy House in Anchorage. It's a group home for girls who've been abused."

Cole looked over at her, surprised to find her eyes staring at the moon, the bright light rimming her pupils like cut glass.

"It wasn't my daddy. He'd never do anything like that. He's just an alcoholic. It was two of his army friends. They were all drunk and when Daddy passed out, they got overly friendly in the kitchen, touching me in *inappropriate* ways. That's what they call it at the home. My mama sent me there because I was cutting myself."

Hannah held up her arm to Cole, ran her finger down a ladder of thin scars. "I don't do that anymore. I know how to take care of myself now."

"What did your mother say when you told her about the soldiers?"

"She's a born-again Christian. Those kinds of things don't happen in her world."

Those things shouldn't happen in any world, Cole thought, and through all his righteous indignation over the inexcusable act, he suddenly felt just as guilty, just as unforgivable. He harbored similar thoughts, imagining Hannah's skin beneath his rough fingertips, the warmth at the splice of her legs. Inappropriate. But far worse. Appalling.

Cole set the half-finished beer on the railing of the porch and hiked up his trousers. "I've got to go," he said. "I won't be back."

"I'm leaving in a few days anyway," she said.

That's when Cole knew he had lied to himself, and Hannah. He was disappointed she was leaving, that he would never see her again, yet he had convinced himself he'd never return to Hannah's house, to Turnback Creek, that he was finished thinking about her. Cole nodded, his legs suddenly unsteady, empty. Every parting gesture—a handshake, a hug, a "Nice to meet you"—seemed awkward, unsuitable. He didn't know how to say good-bye to the girl.

"What's your sister's name?" Hannah asked.

"Elsie."

Hannah nodded, then tilted the beer back and finished the last of it. She turned toward the house, stopping on the porch to sit in the rocker. She didn't look over at Cole, just stared out across the lawn.

Cole glanced back a few times before he reached the edge of the woods, Hannah's silhouette and the porch growing smaller, her profile fixed against the shadows. He expected something else, expected her to speak to him once again before he reached the trees, expected to hear the rumble of the backhoe loader starting. He turned back one last time, almost expecting to see himself still crossing the field, as if he had left some significant part of himself behind. Nothing but grass stood between him and the house. Hannah was gone, the porch vacant, the windows dark.

When Cole pushed the boat away from the bank, he noticed the ripple on the water, felt the breeze from the back of the cove. He fired the outboard, shoved the throttle into gear, and spun the boat sharply toward the mouth of Turnback Creek.

## *Chapter 7*

Ms. Corbett led Lily from Elsie's bedroom just as Cole entered the living room. He'd seen Ms. Corbett's car in the driveway, all the lights in the house on, and figured something was wrong. And by the tears tracking down Lily's cheeks, Cole knew Elsie was dead. Ms. Corbett's smile was soft and reassuring. Lily collapsed in the lounger, cradling her face in her hands.

"Elsie is peaceful now, Mr. Emerson. I called the hospital and an ambulance is coming directly."

Cole eased past her, pausing a moment to touch Lily's shoulder. Lily reached up to grab his hand, letting his fingers slip through hers as he headed for the back bedroom.

"Did she say anything?" he asked, speaking to Lily but looking at the carpet.

Lily shook her head. "No, Daddy. I just went to check on her and she was gone, her blankets on the floor."

Cole nodded and went to Elsie's side.

His mind had been a restless tangle on the boat ride from Turnback Creek to home and a part of him had sensed that Elsie had died, even though he wouldn't have been able to state it as such. The notion hadn't burst into consciousness like a well-formed picture the way he imagined it did for those psychic folks. No, it had just eased across him slowly, like a humid summer night, a sticky dread without source or clarity. At first he'd thought it was about Hannah, and maybe part of it had been—the way the girl had tilted back her beer like a man hot and sweaty from hard work, or the casualness with which she spoke of burying a man under tons of concrete and rebar—but it was more than Hannah, it was the memory of the day his father had left. There had been something different that day, something he hadn't been able to pin down exactly until the boat ride across Hardman Lake.

Walking in from school that day, he found the house almost too still, Elsie's muted sobs filling the stairwell. Everything that day had been extreme in its subtlety, to the point that it was hard not to notice. Elsie had never cried when their daddy left at other times. Maybe she had been too young to understand, or maybe she knew he'd be back. Yet this time she couldn't seem to stop crying. And their mama had always assured them he'd be back, that he was just away on business, or had some urgent matter to attend to in the next county, and she had always told them with eyes still red and puffy from crying, which made it difficult for Cole to believe at the time, even though his daddy always returned just like she said. But that was the part that now bothered Cole. His mother had always cried when his father left, wailing and pleading to God at first, then sobbing at the kitchen sink, her back to the table, her face bent toward the sudsy water so far it looked like she didn't have a head on her shoulders. But not that day. She hadn't pleaded to anyone and her eyes were dry as autumn wheat.

Cole leaned over Elsie's body, grasped her hand, and was surprised by the weight of it, the cool clay feeling of her flesh. Elsie had stayed in her room the entire afternoon after their father left, even though Cole had knocked and pestered her to let him in.

"Leave her be," his mother had said. "I've got chores for you in the garden."

"Is it Papa? Is that why she's so upset? Does she think he's not coming back?" he had asked. "He'll come back. Papa always does."

"Spread this blood meal around the plants," his mother had told him, handing him the tin bucket.

Once in the garden, he'd picked up small stones and tossed them at Elsie's window. Elsie peered out one time, her face pale as a plate, then disappeared. Her face was just as colorless now, but softer, the creases at the corners of her mouth and eyes taken by death. Cole thought it strange that death somehow made Elsie look younger.

"You could bury a man where no one would ever find him." Cole was thinking about Hannah, what she'd said earlier that night, then about everything Elsie had said to Lily over the past few days. He thought back to how Elsie refused to play in the barn after their daddy left, how Candy Bar bucked and protested her stall until he'd had to put her in another. He thought about the calm reserve in his mother's face that day, how she'd handed him the bucket of blood meal and peered unblinking into his eyes until he'd had to look away, uncomfortable with the solid weight of her gaze. He wondered what he'd find if he took a backhoe loader to Candy Bar's stall, dug up the dirt like he'd done at the Noble Church Cemetery in Louisiana fifty years ago. Would he hear the crunch of bones long buried and stained with dirt and blood as the teeth of the steel bucket gouged into the earth? He wondered who owned the land now, and was the barn still standing? Was it covered over with a shopping mall, or an asphalt parking lot, or impounded under acres of water?

Cole felt a hand on his shoulder and turned to see Lily. She wore the worried smile of a small child. "I didn't know what to do, Daddy. She wasn't moving. Her lips were purple."

"You did just fine," Cole said, picturing his father under all that dirt, under all that time.

Lily squeezed his hand. "I'm glad you came back, Daddy."

Lonnie Busch's short stories have appeared or are forthcoming in such publications as *The Minnesota Review*, *The Baltimore Review*, *Chicago Quarterly Review*, The *Southeast Review*, *Talking River Review*, *Flint Hills Review*, *The Iconoclast*, *Pisgah Review*, *MoonShine Review*, and others. Stories of his have also been finalists in the World's Best Short Short Story Competition in 2004, The Tobias Wolff Award for Fiction in 2005, and most recently, the *Glimmer Train* Very Short Fiction Award. As a painter, illustrator, Busch has created artwork for corporations and institutions across the United States, including the 2002 "Greetings from America" stamps and the 2004 "Summer Olympics" stamp for the US Postal Service. His most recent projects include the cover for Jimmy Buffett's latest novel, *A Salty Piece of Land*, as well as a block of forty new stamps for the Postal Service, entitled "Wonders of America," in May of 2006